The Penalty

The Penalty

MAL PEET

CANDLEWICK PRESS

Copyright © 2007 by Mal Peet

First U.S. paperback edition in this format 2016

The Library of Congress has cataloged the hardcover edition as follows:

Peet, Mal.
The penalty / Mal Peet. — 1st U.S. ed.
p.   cm.
Summary: Paul Faustino, known as the best soccer journalist in the business, reluctantly investigates the disappearance of eighteen-year-old Ricardo, a soccer prodigy known as "El Brujito," while in alternate chapters a slave in old San Juan becomes a powerful voodoo priest.
ISBN 978-0-7636-3399-8 (hardcover)
[1. Missing persons — Fiction.   2. Journalists — Fiction.
3. Voodooism — Fiction.   4. Slavery — Fiction.
5. Soccer — Fiction.   6. South America — Fiction
7. South America — History. — To 1806 — Fiction.]   I. Title.
PZ7.P3564 Pen 2007
[Fic] — dc22   2007022112

ISBN 978-0-7636-4339-3 (paperback)
ISBN 978-0-7636-8747-2 (reformatted paperback)

16 17 18 19 20 21 BVG 10 9 8 7 6 5 4 3 2 1

Printed in Berryville, VA, U.S.A.

This book was typeset in Horley Old Style MT.

Candlewick Press
99 Dover Street
Somerville, Massachusetts 02144

visit us at www.candlewick.com

In memory of Miles Davis,
who ran the voodoo down

PROLOGUE: DEVOTION

You would think the boy is alone, but he is not. Facing him is the Brazilian defense. That plastic beer crate is Michel. The little heap of stones is Luisao, who today is holding the center. The almost-leafless sapling that grows magically out of nothing is the magisterial Cafu. The ancient bicycle frame propped up with bricks is Maicon, whose ferocious tackling is legendary. Beyond them, between the two thin timbers the boy has somehow uprighted in the hard earth, lurks the goalkeeper, Rubinho. He will be substituted for Cesar at halftime, but that will make no difference. The boy knows he can beat them both. He can drive the ball in a powerful curve that will take it a finger's breadth inside the post. He can send in a long-distance shot that seems destined to fly over the invisible bar but that will dip horribly at the last possible moment. He can do these things, and more, but often does not bother. He is less interested in the final shot than in the move that leads up to it. In the beauty of the move, in its speed and complexity.

And the boy is not alone, because — as always — his head is full of spirits with whom he talks and in whom he confides.

Nor is he lonely. He practices in solitude because the other boys are not as good as he is. Their failure to understand what he intends to do frustrates him. They are slow to read the game. They fail to predict what the Brazilians will do. And they are not serious. They want only to score goals so that they can celebrate with their ridiculous gymnastics, reveling in the silent roar of eighty thousand imaginary spectators.

The ball the boy bounces from knee to knee is old, cheap, and scuffed. In places the plastic coating is peeling away. He knows that soon, somehow, he will have to get another one. But in the meantime, the sad condition of the ball makes the game a little more unpredictable, and he likes that.

The boy's field is a large patch of bare, uneven ground where once, long ago, a church stood. He has set up the goal where the altar used to be, although he does not know this. Since the destruction of the church, nothing has been built here because the place is considered unlucky. He is aware of this, feels the wrongness that lingers in the air, but he welcomes it because bad luck is part of any game. It is something else to test himself against.

4

He catches the ball on his instep, holds it there for five seconds, and begins another attack. After a burst of extremely sudden acceleration that takes Michel by surprise, he plays a one-two with a low chunk of broken masonry, the stump of a wall. The return pass is perfectly weighted; it evades Luisao's desperate attempt at interception, and the ball drops into a space that Michel will not reach in time. The boy takes it on the outside of his right foot and sets off on a direct run toward the center of the penalty area, and, as he had intended, the Brazilians funnel in toward the goal, their eyes on the ball. But he does not continue the run. Instead he brakes, comes to a dead stop. The ball is, tantalizingly, a pace in front of his right foot; it tempts Maicon, who closes in, his face almost blank with determination. And the boy, with outrageous insolence, plays it through the defender's legs. There is only just enough room between the V of the bicycle frame and its crossbar for the ball to pass through—but it does pass through and runs out wide to where the boy's fullback is making an overlapping run. When the pass comes in, it is sweetly hit, with some inswing, and the boy meets it with his head.

Or he would have.

His name is Ricardo Gomes de Barros, and he is fourteen years old. His aunt, with whom he lives—he has no parents, although he sometimes hears their voices in his head—calls him Rico. So does his sister. The other kids, the ones who call him anything at all, call him El Brujito. The Little Magician. The Little Sorcerer. Because he can do impossible things, such as disappear. Turn the wrong way onto a ball, fake you out, and be gone. A minute later, he will reappear in a place where he cannot possibly be. He can take the ball on his chest with his back to you, and even if you charge into him and knock him down, you will not find the ball. You will look around for it only to discover that it has somehow found its way to another forward who has outflanked your entire defense. There is perhaps something supernatural about Brujito's ability to do these things. And he himself would not deny it. Not out of arrogance, but out of modesty.

He is wearing a Deportivo San Juan soccer jersey. Its red and black quarters have faded, and it is ripped at the seam below both armpits. One of his imitation Adidas sneakers is splitting along the seam of the upper and the sole, and the lace of the other has been replaced by green nylon string. The sky above him is pearl white, already pinkish above the tree line. Soon other boys will drift by, and some will call out to him.

"Hey, Brujito! Chill, man! Come on down to the boat shed!"

"Yeah, c'mon, freak! Jaco's got some wicked smoke!"

He will lift a thumb and say, "Cool. See you later maybe."

But he won't go, even though it is rumored that Rafael's sister will be there tonight and they say she will do anything.

And in a vague and troubling way, he is curious to discover what *anything* is.

The broken-down, patched-up, and doorless building where the kids gather at night is still called the boat shed because in over two hundred years no one has bothered to think of anything else to call it. The lower, original parts of its walls are built of massive blocks of chiseled stone that are now green with hairy moss; thick-rooted ferns grow in their cracks. The boat shed faces onto the rough asphalt dockside. Beyond that, the jetty steps out into the river, its stout old legs gartered with weed.

The kids will rig up a sound system and play American hip-hop. They'll maybe light a trash fire in a cut-down oil barrel. They'll open cans of Coke, swig from them, then top them up with rough cheap *cachaza*. They'll pass around joints, exclaiming theatrically when they exhale. Lately, some of the older boys have been bringing crack down from the city, impressing the younger ones with the dexterity with which they fashion pipes out of aluminum foil.

But he won't go. There are several reasons for this.

He is not disliked, but he is not popular. Most of the boys share his fanaticism about soccer, but they cannot share his devotion to its arts. It's too much. They've all watched the soap operas, the ones where some dirt-poor, screwed-up kid who happens to be a soccer genius is discovered in some crappy little town like this one and goes on to win the World Cup, or something stupid like that. And they know it's just

TV. Another kind of dope. But El Brujito *believes* in it, man. Like he's actually *getting ready for it to happen.* Crazy. Weird. He's OK, but OK like that sorry kid Paolo whose brain is wrong. Harmless, but not someone you'd be down with. And then there's all that religious stuff he's into. Same as his kid sister. It comes from being brought up by that loco aunt of his, with her back-to-Africa Veneration thing. Dressing up in that old-style Looney Tunes white outfit, speaking in tongues, the rest of that crap. Not his fault, but . . .

The girls aren't into him. He's a bit on the short side, and stocky. He has this set to his face that makes him look sort of angry, even when he isn't. Or like he's concentrating on something that no one else knows about. His skin has a reddish undertone to it, like mahogany. It's not the beautiful rich black Rigo has, which sometimes looks blue in certain kinds of light. Nor is it the burnt honey color that Nelson has, which is gorgeous. He doesn't know what to say to you if you don't want to talk about soccer. He sweats. He doesn't take any trouble with his hair. He isn't cool, and the thing is, it's like he doesn't want to be.

So although the other kids call to him, ask him down to the session, it's more of a windup than an invitation. They know he won't come. And he knows they know.

There is one reason above all others that he will not go down to the boat shed: his spirits are against it. His spirit ancestor is Achache, the Magician, the Dancer. Achache does not want him to use the stuff they use down there.

Achache speaks frequently of what happened to Diego Maradona: how the greatest soccer genius in the world killed his spirit with pleasurable poisons and turned himself into a toad. The boy does not dare offend Achache because he knows it is from him that he derives his skill.

And behind Achache, greater than Achache, is Maco, the Judge. The boy has never seen Maco clearly. Very few people have. He has caught glimpses, as if through darkened glass; as far as the boy can tell, Maco doesn't much resemble the image at the center of the shrine in his aunt's best room. He knows, though, that if Maco judges you offside, there is no appeal. Maco cannot be appeased. If he is against you, you can never win. He will separate you from your soul and turn you ghost. Brujito therefore avoids anything that Maco might disapprove of. He wears a DSJ shirt because they are the local team, the team he will one day play for, but by a coincidence that cannot be a coincidence, red and black are also Maco's colors.

He begins again. There is a move—a stop and turn—that he needs to perfect. He's got it down, more or less, but he's not breaking out of it fast enough. He pushes the ball ahead of him with the underside of his foot and glances up at the opposition. This time he'll try it against Cafu, yes. As he begins his run, he hears the first beats of the boom box sounding over the slow green river that winds through a forest he doesn't know the limits of.

ONE: CARRYING FIRE

We were river people, fishermen. People of the river spirit, Loma, who is slow and green and clever. We were not warriors, so when the fierce people from beyond the forest attacked our village, we did not know what to do. They came out of the trees, howling, at the time of light-but-no-sun-yet, when my mother and the other women were waking the first fires.

I picked up my young sister, who was playing at the front of our house, and ran with the others toward our boats. Some of us fell with spears in our backs. I looked for my mother and saw her go down broken beneath the feet of the fierce people who swept over her like water. And when we reached the sands, we saw two great war canoes on the river, and in them there were terrible No-Skins who killed more of us with their fire sticks. My father was one who died there. He went onto his knees with his hands on his chest full of blood, and then he fell with his face in the water. The air was so full of screaming that I could hardly breathe it. We were trapped, and I thought we would all die, and I tried to make myself ready. But they did not kill us. Not there, not then.

The war canoes came onto the beach, breaking our boats. The fierce people and the No-Skins used their spears and their fire sticks to beat the women and children back toward the houses. They tore my sister from me. She did not cry out even when they threw her down, but her eyes were huge and her mouth was open like a person found drowned.

I was kneeling beside my father, chanting for his spirit, when I looked up and saw a No-Skin looking down at me. His face was the color of a peeled animal with the fat still on it, but there was yellow fur around his mouth.

That was how I thought then: peeled animal, yellow fur, fire sticks. Because I had never seen white men before or their guns.

I was terribly afraid. I thought the one standing over me was Lord Death from our stories. He kept his raw-looking eyes on me and shouted in his language. Hands seized me and forced me to where our other men had been gathered. Our hands were tied together and our necks fastened to a long chain of iron.

That is how I was stolen—even though I was fourteen years old and would not be a man for another three parts of a year.

♦   ♦   ♦

We walked for many days, many days. Four white men and some fierce people came with us. If we fell, they beat us. Once a day, they fed us a terrible porridge like vomit. At night they made us sleep without coverings on the ground, so we woke up cold and wet. Three of us died of the shivering sickness. The white men cut them free of the chain and left them alone in the forest without any ceremonies, and this filled the rest of us with so much fear that we tried very hard not to die.

Then at last we came to the top of a hill made of sand, and I saw ahead of me that the sky was cut in two, the lower half darker and full of small white running clouds. It was the sea, and in my ignorance I thought it was beautiful.

When we saw the white men's ship, we were struck with terror, not knowing what it was. My thought was: this is their object of worship. Because huge skeletons stood on it, hung with sheets the color of death. And I thought I knew why we had been brought here. To be sacrifice. To be fed to this god of theirs. And in a way I was right.

Sometimes in my village, when the men pulled in the nets, there would be many small fish as well as the good fat ones. These small fish we called *panga usha*, babies' fingers. We did not throw them away. When the catch had been sorted, the women packed the *panga usha* into tubs made of tree bark. There was a way of doing it. First, a circle of fish around the bottom of the tub with their noses against the side. Then another circle, noses against the tails of the first circle of fish. And so on, fish nose to tail, smaller and smaller circles, until the bottom was covered. Then the women would cover this layer with sweet-smelling leaves and start again. Another layer of fish, nose to tail, more leaves. Many layers. When the barrel was full, heavy pieces of wood went on top; then it was buried in the sand. On ancestor days, the barrels were dug up and we would eat the fish. Now their bones were soft and their flesh was sweet.

That was how the whites packed us into their ship, head to toe. We lay there with our mouths open and eyes wide in the darkness, like *panga usha,* waiting to be eaten. But the layers between us were not sweet leaves. They were floors of wood that smelled of human filth.

I do not know how many we were. There were some that we knew, from other villages along the river. There were also many Other People, who had very dark skins and did not speak our language. We were all mixed up together. There were some women too, but they were packed into another part of the ship.

We lay in fearful silence for a long time. There was no light to reckon the day by. Then there was shouting, and many hard feet passing above our heads, and a terrible clatter like rocks being tumbled down a stream in flood. The wooden walls all around and above groaned and screeched, and everything tilted one way. Our bodies rolled onto each other. The darkness was full of clutching hands and flying chains and limbs all mixed together with howls of pain and terror. I thought that if this violent burial lasted an hour, half an hour, we would all be dead.

It lasted fifty-two days.

It was not long before we started dying. I think some of the Other People made themselves die. They closed their eyes and would not eat or drink. Then the emptying sickness began. The stink was terrible. The white men covered their faces with cloth when they went down to carry the bodies out.

I survived because after five days I was taken out of the belly of the ship. A white man, the one who cooked the food, befriended me. His name was Billywells. He called me Little Macaque. I slept inside the shack at the back of the ship, where he worked, and in the morning and just before darkness, I crawled among our people with the food tubs and the water barrel and the cup. The white men did not like to do this because of the heat and the stink, and because they were afraid, even though our people were chained together and one could not move unless all the others moved at the same time.

Because I was on the roof of the ship, I saw what happened to our dead bodies. They were thrown into the sea, naked as they were born and with no ceremonies. Sometimes, even though their spirits had left them, they would not go down but would lie in the water with their faces to the sky. On days of no wind, they would stay against the walls of the ship, like logs that gathered together at the slow places on our river.

Some of the white men died too, when the emptying sickness moved among them. But with them it was different. The body was sewn tight into strong cloth to protect it, and gifts of iron were put in with it. The other white men came together around the body and did ceremonies of worship and chanting. So when it was put in the sea, it went down under the water and did not come back up. I thought that was where the white ancestors lived, at the bottom of the sea.

The way our bodies were treated filled me with so much fear and worry that it was like having a snake living in me. I knew that one of the men down in the belly of the ship was a *pai*, a priest. I spoke with him, whispering. I asked him if the spirits of those put in the sea would be able to find their way home.

He said, "No, they will not."

"Can you not help them, Pai?"

He said, "I am not your *pai* here. I have no powers here."

There were tears running from his eyes.

Two days later at watering time, he spoke to me again, saying, "I have been dreaming. Put your ear against my mouth."

I did, and he said, "The white men are taking us to their country, which I cannot picture. When you get there, you must speak to the ancestors so that they know where we are and can fetch us."

This made me shake. I said, "I do not understand, Pai. How can I speak to the ancestors? I do not know how. I am not from a wise family. Can you not do this?"

He turned his head away from me. I could see all the bones beneath his skin.

"No," he said. "I have seen that I will not be there. You must do it. I will teach you how."

I thought I would live this death forever. Wander this water desert forever. A numbness soaked into me so that I thought I was going ghost. Sometimes I looked at my hands, my feet, and wondered with not much interest who they belonged to.

In my first life, when I had a home, I learned from my mother the skill of making a carrying fire. While my father and uncles prepared the big boat, I would pick the slowest and strongest embers from our cooking fire and wrap them in leaves. First a little dry litter to feed them, then wrappings of oily leaves, then wrappings of the thick green leaves that could not burn. Tie the bundle in a clever way with twisted fibers. The fire would sleep in there for a long time. When we had traveled far upriver and it was time to rest and eat, we would open the bundle and wake the fire with our breath.

The *pai* had given me a carrying fire. His teachings. That is why I did not go ghost. That is why I went through death and came out the other side.

One morning I was woken up not by the cold or by the poke of Billywells's foot but by a great clamor of shouting. The white men were very excited. Some danced on the floor of the ship with their arms around each other. Some made a crisscross sign on the front of their bodies.

At first I thought it was just another shadow of rain cloud on the edge of the sea. Then I saw that it did not drift and change. It was land. This land.

There was wind and little sweeps of rain on our backs, and the bellies of the sails were full. By the middle of the day, I could see hills and trees. That night, the ship rested for the first time. There was land ahead and to the side of it, and when the moon rose, I saw a pale line where the water ended. That night too, Billywells brought a barrel to the middle of the ship and pierced it, and it leaked drink into the white men's cups. I hid in the cooking shack when they got fierce and noisy, but Billywells came to me and poured some of the drink into my mouth. It was wet fire, and I thought he was killing me because he had no more use for me. I fought and spat, but some of it burned down into me and my stomach rose up against my ribs. This made Billywells happy, and he rubbed my head and went away shouting.

◆   ◆   ◆

We did not land in that place. The ship sailed close to the shore for two more days. I could smell the trees. And we came at last to a world of stone. A long rampart of stone and wood rose out of the water, almost as high as the walls of the ship. From the top of this rampart a great space stretched away, and the ground was also stone. This space was full of people and all sorts of loud work, and I did not know whether it was a joy or a terror to see that most of the people were black like us, although they wore clothes like the white men. Things I did not know the names of were heaped all around, and there were strange four-legged animals wearing baskets on the sides of their bodies. Also houses of stone. One of them was very big, bigger than any house I had ever seen, with a great gate in it like an open mouth. Then came a gray cliff that reached up to the sky. And I saw that there was a crooked road climbing the cliff, and people and the basket animals were going up and down it in lines like leaf ants in the forest.

When our men and women were brought out of the belly of the ship, some of them moaned in fear when they saw where they were. But many were too weak even to cry out, and some had the big-eye sickness and could see nothing. Many had legs that would not unfold, and they had to be carried from the ship on hammocks hung between two poles. Black people did the carrying, and some of us tried to speak with them, but they would not answer. Some of them were weeping. I still had strength because I had not been chained and because of the extra food that Billywells had given me. So I was made to carry a man in my arms down onto the hot stone earth. He was taller than me and bigger, but he was like bent sticks with a head. He weighed almost nothing, but I staggered and almost dropped him. My legs had forgotten how to walk on level ground.

We were taken into the mouth of the big house. Other people were in there already, among the shadows, and when they saw us, they sang and mourned.

We were there for many days. We slept on dry grass, and we had coverings at night. White men came and looked closely at us and gave us bitter medicines. Also food, not only the filthy porridge but strange fruits and bird meat and a kind of bread. Most of us lived. We learned to walk again, growing stronger.

And when we were strong enough to bear it, the white men burned a mark on the front of our shoulders with a red-hot iron.

The day came when we were taken up the crooked road that climbed the cliff. We were all joined together by a chain, and this made the walking difficult. Stones bit our feet. On one side of the road, there was only airy nothingness and a great fall, which filled me with a kind of drifting sickness when I looked at it. We climbed so high that we were level with the great black birds that sailed across the face of the rock, turning their gray heads to look at us.

When we reached the top of the cliff, many of us cried out in fear and wonder, because we found ourselves in a great city of stone houses that filled our sight, and they were magical colors, and some had towers that were taller than the masts of the death ship. And what marveled me was that light burned from many of the windows, so bright that I could not look. I thought these houses must have their own suns trapped inside them. This was the first time I saw glass, a thing I came to love. Sheets of nothing that you can touch, and see through without being seen. Like the thin invisible wall you step through if you die.

And the towering city of colored stone was full of people. Black people like us and white people. It took some time for me to understand that the white people who had no legs, who floated in great robes, were women, because the robes covered their breasts. As we climbed the last steps, the sky filled with the sound of bells and many people came toward us, calling out in their languages and pointing. They surrounded us like a cloud of bright-colored flies when we were led along the hot stone road between the houses. We were almost naked. We had been given small aprons of cloth, which hardly covered our sexual parts, and the women stared at us, hiding the lower parts of their faces behind little screens like painted palm leaves. And I saw that there were black women who did the same, and who wore long robes like the whites, and my mind struggled to understand this.

In a great sloping space between the houses, we were chained to a wall by our necks and hands and feet. There was a roof of dry grass above our heads, shading us from the sun, who was in a cruel mood. We were all croaking our thirst, and after some time we were given water. Things were done to us. Many people came to touch us, our arms, our legs, our sexual parts. A man pushed my head back and forced my mouth open and looked into it. When he had gone, the bitter taste of his fingers lasted a long time.

Then a white man and a black man stood in front of us. The black man beat a blood-red drum, and the white man held a long black stick in the air. His face was covered in sweat so that it looked like a mask of polished wood with black eye-holes. The crowd became silent. He spoke to them in a great voice, then came close to us. He laid his stick on the shoulder of the first man chained to the wall, and when he did so, many of the white people in the crowd called out and lifted their arms. There was much shouting and sometimes laughter like barking. Then there was a quietness; the black man struck his drum, and the white man made marks on a paper.

I was the fourth in the line, and when the stick touched me, all the eyes of all the people also touched me. It was the first time in my life so many people had looked at me, and the power of their looking made me tremble so much I thought my legs would fail and I would fall and choke on the iron collar that clutched my throat. Then it was over and the white man made his marks on the paper and moved his stick to the man chained next to me.

When we had all been touched and shouted at, the white man went among the crowd, leaving the man with the drum close to us. He looked at me and spoke quietly in a language I did not understand.

Then he looked more closely at me and used a different

language, wonderfully my own. "Loma person? From the great river?"

I nodded, feeling my heart grow big as prayer. I saw now that behind the drum and beneath the white man clothes there was a boy not much older than myself.

He said, "You belong now to Colonel d'Oliviera. It could be worse."

I was silenced because I understood his words but not his meaning.

"His place is two days' boat from here."

Still I could find nothing to say. He looked to see where the white man with the stick was, then turned his face back to me. "Who is your ancestor?"

I answered, "Achache."

"The Dancer," he said.

"And the Magician."

He looked at the ground between us, then lifted his face. "It would be best if you forgot him. Worship is useless here. We are beyond reach. Not even great Maco knows where we are. I have seen things that teach me this. Soon you will see them too."

I licked my lips. I could not tell him about the *pai* and the burden of his knowledge that I carried.

He said, "The white shits call this place El Mundo Nuevo, the New World. And they are right. There is nothing old and good here. Listen to me: be who they say you are and try not to die. That is all you can do."

"What is your name?" I asked him.

But before he could answer, the white man with the stick came toward us calling, "Jaquito! Jaquito!"

The boy bared his teeth at me, a smile that was not a smile.

"That is what they call me," he said, and turned away and played a summons on his drum.

And then we stood in our chains and watched the whippings. We mourned and groaned because we had never seen such a thing done to men. Each one was tied to a rack like the ones we dried our nets on, back in the real life. Each one screamed and prayed when the first lashes struck him and then fell silent because—I thought—he had died. Blood ran down to the ground, and the skin on each back peeled away like the bark of the coloba tree.

I was one of six men bought by Colonel d'Oliviera that day. One of the others was called Abela, and he was also from the great river, although not from my village. We were taken to a yard with iron bars over the windows, where we slept. The next morning a white man came. His hair was greased tight to his skull and tied at the back with a cord made of skin. His nose was long and red and hooked, like a fish hawk's beak. His eyes worried me. They looked like he had been weeping tears of blood. And I had seen him before. The day before. He had stood at the front of the crowd when we were sold.

The black man who had watched over us in the night jumped up when he saw the white man and stood straight as a spear, so I thought that this was the colonel who owned me. It was not. It was Captain Morro. The overseer. A word I did not know then but one I grew to know very well, and hate.

He came close and looked at us. He had a smell that was sweet but also rotten. I knew this smell from the death ship. Rum.

Ah, the pleasure I had, killing him. The richness of the smell in the forest, after the rains. The birds celebrating the new weather. How the life came out of him in thick slow bubbles as I knelt on his shoulders to drown him in the brown water. And then I poured the rum on him and put the bottle in his hand.

This was years later. But for me time is folded, like cloth.

We were given clothes. Breeches and a shirt. It was stiff, the shirt, and harsh on my body until my sweat softened it. Then we walked in chains through the baking crowded streets of stone back to the edge of the cliff. Climbing down was worse than the climbing up. Abela went first. I tried to look only at his back because I was afraid the fainting sickness would take me. But halfway down, I saw that at the foot of the cliff there was a great quarrel of the black birds. They fought and lifted and fell again, too many to count. And when at last we got to the bottom of the road, I saw the reason for their business. A body, one of ours, lay burst in a gully, and they were tearing at it. The eyes had gone and the face was a red mash. I felt a coldness in my blood, which frightened me. Later this coldness would be my power, but I did not know it then.

31

Again we were put on a boat. It was difficult, because they would not release us from the chains and we had to climb down an iron ladder with our faces to the wall. The boat was not much longer than a war canoe, but wider. It had a small sail, bundled on the mast like the white funeral clothes on a thin old woman. Four black men, two on each side, holding oars. At the front, a white man with black fur on his face sat watching us, a gun across his folded legs and another one beside him. With his arms he told us to sit.

We waited a long time while things we did not understand happened. Then Morro climbed down the iron ladder, shouting up at people who stood above us. Sacks and bundles were handed down with a great amount of fuss and argument. The boat rocked and banged against the wall. Morro at last sat himself in a shelter made of cloth at the back of the boat. He had a glass bottle in his hand, half full of golden liquid.

At first the men rowed the boat. Then we passed a tongue of land and the wind and the waves grew. Sprays of water like thin rain landed on our skins, and the boat shuddered. I saw that Abela was afraid. The four men took their oars from the water and laid them down, then two of them untied the cords around the sail and it opened with a sound like thunder-crack, but softer. The boat swung and tipped. Abela hung his head between his knees and groaned. Morro shouted orders and pulled at a beam of wood fixed to the back of the boat. The sail filled with wind, and it was as if a

32

great hand lifted us and we flew over the water. Morro drank from his bottle, and then, amazing me, he began to sing.

Our flight across the sea slowed. The sail rippled and banged. Morro called out, and the oarsmen pulled on ropes. The sail swung and filled its belly again. The boat leaned. The waves now came from behind us and broke into small pieces and ran away. I began to see sticks and leaves and sometimes big fruits drift past us, and then thickening streams of different-colored water. When I saw forest on both sides of the boat, I understood. We were on a river. A wide, slow, green river.

My thoughts struggled in my head like a hooked fish. I wanted to believe I was coming home. Perhaps I had been in dream time, taken on a vision journey so I could receive the teachings of the dying *pai*. And now I was waking, returning to share the warning stories of what I had seen. Or perhaps the white men's ship had sailed all the way around the bowl of the world, back to the beginning, and just beyond the next bend, I would see my people waiting to greet me, glad that I had passed my manhood ordeal.

The sail finally slumped and died. The men lashed it into bundles again and bent to their oars. I looked at Abela and saw that he too was full of wonder, and that home thoughts had tricked him, also, because tears lay in the hollows below his eyes. How cruel hope is, and what a sly hunter.

33

In the afternoon of the second day, the river changed its mood. I had slept through most of the morning so that the ache of remembering would not go on. I saw that although we seemed to be still in the same place, the water had coils in it and a rougher skin. The sky was gray like light shining on a knife. I smelled rain coming. Ahead of us, small islands covered in low bushes divided the river. I remember thinking it would be a good place to fish. Now the men broke their rhythm to let the river carry the boat closer to the trees. Then they would dig deep into the water, their muscles hard beneath their skins, and we would swing out again. They had good skill. But Morro had been rum-drunk the night before and sat slumped with his arm on the steering beam, looking as if he had eaten bitter fruit.

◆　◆　◆

We were close to a low island made of sand and small stones when the rain came down on us. It was good, steep rain, and I lifted my face to let it run into my mouth. Then something punched the bottom of the boat. The men lifted their oars and called out. Everything tipped. I thought of the terrifying Big Mouth that walked underwater in Loma's river, and fear rose in my throat.

But it was not that. We had wandered from the deep water, and the belly of the boat had run onto the soft floor of the river. It was Morro's fault, and he tried to hide his shame inside anger. With shouts and kicks, he drove us to one side of the boat while the oarsmen used their oars like poles on the other side. It seemed to work. The stern came free and drifted out, but then it was seized by the current. In a heartbeat, the boat swung around, its nose still stuck in the mud. Morro roared and fell upon the steering beam, but it was too late, and the oarsmen who now rushed to our side were blocked by our bodies and all was a confusion of arms and legs and chains. Now we were pointing back the way we had come, and in the grip of the river. Then another great blow to the belly of the boat, and it stopped again. The gunman stumbled and would have fallen on top of us if he had not wrapped one arm around the mast. I looked down into the water and saw swirls of mud and dark tangles of underwater grass. The only sounds were the hiss and prickle of the rain falling onto the river.

Morro stood up. Water dripped from his chin and beak.

He kicked the boat and said the same word many times. *Mierda, mierda, mierda*. The same word he used for us. *Shit*.

Morro looked down at us with his bloodstained eyes. He spoke, but not to us, because the gunman replied. We knew Morro did not like the answer, because he roared the same words again. The gunman lifted his shoulders, then opened a box and took out a hammer and a thick iron pin. He gave them to Morro, who stooped and seized Abela's arm. He laid it on the edge of the boat, then used the hammer and the pin to drive the bolt free of the iron bracelet on Abela's wrist. The chain fell away. Abela was now divided from the rest of us. Strangely, I felt a kind of sadness. Then Morro took my arm and used the hammer and pin to free me from the next man. Abela and I looked up at Morro, trying to understand his shouts and signs. We could not. The rain was thick now and cloaked his words and everything around us. It seemed that he wanted us to stand, so we stood. He showed his teeth and pushed us, and we fell backward into the water. It smacked us with a soft warm hand, like a mother.

The boat was heavy, not like my people's boats. Abela and I heaved at it with our hands and shoulders while Morro cursed down on us. The water was up to our armpits and the mud ran away beneath our feet. The oarsmen pushed against the riverbed and signaled strength and courage, but we could not understand their words, and sometimes when we moved to a new position, we sank deep and could find nothing to stand on. I worried because I knew the full strength of the river was waiting to carry the boat away like a leaf.

It happened suddenly. The bow swung out. I looked up and saw the gunman's face pass above me, his mouth a red hole in its fur. Then there was nothing but water beneath me and the great weight of the boat sliding onto me, forcing me under. I sucked in a breath, saw Abela vanish, then I was in almost-darkness.

I learned then that the spirit of this river was not like Loma. It had a savage playfulness, and its water was full of strong, thin fingers. They snatched and dragged at me when I had kicked free of the boat's shadow, and it took all my strength to escape them and climb into the air. The boat was already a spear-throw away from me. I heard shouts through the rain, saw Morro crouched at the stern, his arm raised, saw the oarsmen struggling to turn the boat into the current. I spread myself in the water and worked my legs. The clothes made me heavy. I thought that death and freedom were both close to me, but I could not choose between them. Then I thought of Abela, and I lifted myself and turned this way and that, but I could not see him.

When I was facing the boat again, it was much closer, as if by some magic. A snake fell from the air and hit the water close to me. A rope. I reached it and held it, turning on my back to breathe what air there was between the river and the rain. I felt something hard and warm strike my legs, and I cried out, choking water.

Abela rose up close to me with death in his face. He may have known me, because he raised his arm with the iron bracelet on it. I tried to reach him with my hand, but I could not and he was gone.

I pulled myself along the rope until hands grasped me, and then I was kneeling on the floor of the boat. The oarsmen had steadied it now, holding it skillfully into the current. Morro and the other white man were staring into the rain. The four chained men looked at me with eyes like moons. Then Morro shouted and pointed. The river and the rain were green smoke and gray smoke. Close to where they met and melted, I saw something black for a moment. A head and a raised arm. Or the branch of a drifting tree that vanished.

The two white men shouted and snarled at each other. Morro seized the gunman by his shirt and raised his fist, but the gunman pulled away and went to the front of the boat, kicking me out of his way. I fell against the legs of the oarsmen and wanted to stay there and sleep or die. But I was taken by the front of my shirt and pulled up. Morro's face was close to mine. It was like the mask of an evil spirit with the hair painted on and yellow teeth in the twisted mouth and some terrible animal looking through the eye-holes. He howled at me, then before I saw it coming, his fist struck my face. My head filled with noisy light, and the brown taste of blood flooded my mouth. I fell to my knees, and when I put my hand to my face, I knew that my lip was in two parts.

◆　◆　◆

The rain stopped late in the day. The sun returned, a ball of red fire hanging low above the river. So when I saw Santo Tomas for the first time, the big white house on the hill seemed stained with diluted blood, like my clothes.

There was full darkness when the boat reached the dock, and men with flaming torches stood above us. I climbed up toward them in chains and began another life.

Two: A Guide to San Juan

From where Paul Faustino stood, there was possibly the best view that San Juan had to offer. Which, in his opinion, wasn't saying much. Many of the old colonial houses around the steeply sloping plaza had been restored, or at least given a coat of paint. Confectioner's colors, mostly: candy pink, pistachio green, marzipan yellow. The blue-and-white bell towers of the Church of Our Lady of the Good Death were quite impressive in a doll's house sort of way. And because the Old City had been built at the top of the cliff, you couldn't see the squalor, ancient and modern, of the port far below. Beyond the tumble of rooftops and churches, there was only the blue division of sea and sky. Photographed from here, San Juan wouldn't look too bad, which was why, Faustino realized, this was the view featured on ninety percent of the postcards you could buy in this otherwise miserable hole.

Faustino's unfavorable opinion of the city of San Juan had been formed long ago. It had nothing to do with the fact that right now he had an iron collar around his neck, iron manacles around his wrists and ankles, and was fastened to a wall by three stout iron chains. The other members of his tour group—two gay Swiss men, a Spanish couple on their honeymoon, three somber African American Baptists, and four intense Japanese—took photographs of him. The guide continued his spiel.

"The terrace we are standing on is called the Old Slave Market. However, the truth is slightly more complicated. For over two hundred years, San Juan was the center of the slave trade in South America. The majority of the houses around this plaza were involved in the selling of slaves. Most of them had walled yards in which slaves were displayed and offered for sale. Only one of these yards still exists, and that will be the next stop on our tour.

"The slaves sold in these houses were mostly women and children, and most were secondhand. Usually their owners did not want to keep them because they were incapable of doing the hard manual work on the sugarcane plantations or tobacco farms. They were not economic. Or perhaps they were troublesome slaves who had run away and been re-captured. They were private sales. Only slaves fresh from Africa were brought up to the terrace for public auction and chained to the wall like this gentleman here."

Faustino tried to bow ironically, but the iron collar bit his throat.

The guide had an identity badge clipped to his shirt pocket—EDSON BAKULA—with a small photograph that did not do him justice. He was, Faustino thought, possibly the most handsome young man he had ever set eyes on. Beautiful, actually. But the habits of a lifetime made Faustino shy away from the word. The truth was, though, that only the guide's good looks could have persuaded Faustino to make such an exhibition of himself. He would never have allowed himself to be chained to a wall by anybody *plain*.

"They were chained like this for two reasons. One was that they were not trusted. It was widely believed that all African men were warriors capable of killing with their hands and feet in ways unknown to white people. This was not true, of course. The second reason was that, after they had been bought, these men were made to witness the terrible punishments that took place in The Pillory, the square in front of us. And it was thought that seeing these sights might make them difficult to control."

The Swiss with the shaved head now asked a question.

Edson Bakula said, unsmiling, "No, they were not entirely naked. The Catholic priests would usually insist that the private parts of the slaves were covered, in case the women in the crowd became . . ." He was stuck for a proper word.

Faustino croaked, "Inflamed?"

"Yes, perhaps," the guide said, with some slight hesitation. "*Inflamed*. Thank you, Señor. Now, I think it is time you were released."

Forty-five minutes later, when the group emerged from the Church of Christ the Redeemer and dispersed, Faustino backtracked to The Pillory and found a bar that claimed to have air-conditioning. The tour guide's rather too vivid descriptions of the whippings and maimings that had taken place in the square had left Faustino feeling both queasy and empty. A cold beer and a toasted sandwich were called for. The bar also sold newspapers, and he bought three: his own paper, La Nación; the regional tabloid, El Norte; and the local weekly, Voz de San Juan. He took them to a table at the back of the room and spread them out. All three, of course, featured prominently the story that had been dominating the news for the last seven days: the sensational and mysterious disappearance of Ricardo Gomes de Barros, otherwise known as El Brujito.

Voz had the headline BRUJITO: THE MYSTERY DEEPENS and a photo of the eighteen-year-old prodigy celebrating a goal. The article recapped the story so far. After missing a penalty during Deportivo San Juan's cup semifinal against underdog Atlético, Brujito had been substituted. He had gone straight to the locker room, apparently in "a state of deep dejection." At the end of the game—which DSJ had lost "in a shock upset"—the disgraced players returned to the locker room to find that Brujito had vanished. At first it was assumed that the young star had been too shamed by his performance to face his teammates or, perhaps, too afraid to face the wrath of his manager, Victor Morientes. But DSJ became extremely worried when after two days they had failed to make contact with their player, and had alerted the police. Now, a week later, there was still no trace of Brujito, despite the fact that the police had "explored every avenue of investigation."

The rest of the piece was padded out with background stuff and quotes. Morientes was "baffled and deeply concerned," while the chief of San Juan's Criminal Investigations Department was "deeply concerned and baffled." Gilberto da Silva, the Deportivo chairman and owner, was "unavailable for comment." No surprise there, Faustino thought. It was his wife, Flora, who did the talking. And wore the pants, for that matter. But it seemed that on this occasion she had nothing to say either.

Faustino's sandwich arrived, and he scanned *El Norte* while he ate. The front page consisted almost entirely of a headline in a huge typeface: BRUJITO RANSOM DEMAND A HOAX—POLICE. For some reason, the color photo that ran down the page was of a nubile girl wearing a bikini made, apparently, from three postage stamps held together by strands of cobweb. Faustino studied it for some time and then turned to the story, which was continued on page three.

47

It seemed obvious to him that this kidnap stuff was what his boss called "life rafting": something thrown in to stop a good story from sinking when there was nothing new to keep it afloat. So he was surprised when he turned finally to *La Nación,* where the Brujito affair had been relegated to the bottom of the front page, below the lead story, which featured the latest atrocity in the Middle East. The piece was captioned: RANSOM DEMAND FOR MISSING SOCCER STAR. The byline read: *From Maximo Salez in San Juan.* Faustino groaned aloud but read the thing anyway. Then he sat brooding, pinching his lower lip with his fingers.

It was a pain in the rear end, to put it mildly. Here he was, the senior sportswriter for the country's biggest paper, the best—no point being modest about it—soccer journalist in the business. And here was this Brujito story, the biggest story since the World Cup. A perfect Paul Faustino story. He was even here, in godforsaken San Juan, right where it was all happening. But he wasn't covering it. Couldn't cover it. Because he was on leave, researching a book he wasn't sure he could write: *Keeper: The Autobiography of El Gato, as Told to Paul Faustino.* A great man, El Gato, certainly the best goalkeeper—or ex-goalkeeper, now—the world had ever seen. But also maybe a liar. Also maybe a nutcase. Mind you, the money . . .

Faustino had been staggered, alarmed even, by the amount the publishers had offered him. The equivalent of two years' salary, upfront, before he'd written a word. He'd taken it, of course. And agreed to deliver the book in six months. Dear God. He lit another cigarette. Nope, he'd have to leave the Brujito story alone. Leave it to half-wit semiliterate hacks like Maximo Salez, and morons who used phrases like "shock upset." Damn!

Faustino looked at his watch: not quite noon. Now that his interview with Cesar Fabian had been delayed a day, an empty afternoon yawned ahead of him. He really ought to visit the Park, that swath of preserved forest where Gato claimed to have seen a ghost. But he didn't want to trek out there, not in this heat. There were the famous churches, of course; San Juan was stuffed with them. Those old slave owners sure loved to build big churches. Amazing what you could do with a bad conscience and plenty of cheap labor. But to hell with churches. Monuments to dread, all of them. If he wanted to depress himself thinking about sin and the insignificance of human life, he could do that right here, without getting off his backside. Two more beers and another look at the newspapers would do the job.

Maybe some sea air, then. Yes, why not?

Faustino walked from The Pillory past the bars and video stores on the Plaza Jesús and joined the line for the public elevator down to the port. In the crowded, plummeting car, he was the only white person. Two children, their faces level with his knees, gazed up at him as if he were a plaster saint that had left its niche in the cathedral wall to go among the poor. At ground level, he was swept by the tide of people out onto the forecourt. Faustino dimly remembered that the quickest route to the harbor was through the great grim building on the far side of the road, the food market. He dodged his way through the fried-fish sellers, the beggars, the blind hawkers of religious trinkets and lottery tickets. He survived the murderous traffic on the boulevard and, passing through the market's great arched entrance, found himself in an avenue lined with raw flesh. On both sides of the aisle, flayed carcasses hung heads-down from hooks, their eyes still wide from shock, their snouts bloody. Between them, festive swags of dark red sausages; below them, steel counters heaped with ears and feet, spongy tripes, and slippery livers. Business was being conducted in a roar of argument and laughter. Faustino hurried through, keeping his eyes fixed on the exit, the archway that framed the blue level of the sea.

The open area between the market and the harbor was crowded with plastic tables and chairs. Faustino found a shaded place at the farthest edge of the throng. A waitress appeared beside him the instant he sat down. He ordered an iced coffee, which, when it came, was better than he'd expected. Smoking, he watched the incessant comings and goings of the ferries carrying humans and other cargo between the islands that lay humped in the bay like gray whales.

Faustino began to relax, relishing the breeze from the sea and enjoying the small dramas and comedies taking place along the docks and jetties, so it irritated him greatly when a familiar and unwelcome rhythm disturbed his peace. At the far side of the café, a small circular stage had been set up. A quartet of musicians stood beside it: two skinny guys in knitted Rasta hats playing hand drums, a kid with a tambourine, an older man tapping at the strings of a kora. The music they produced was light but slow and monotonous, the kind of stuff you might play at a slightly jolly funeral.

Sighing, Faustino leaned back in his chair to watch. Half a

51

dozen slim but muscular young men appeared from some-where and stood alongside the musicians, solemn-faced. They wore pale blue jerseys and shiny yellow tracksuit bot-toms with a green stripe, and were barefoot. At a nod from the old kora player, two of them stepped onto the stage and went into their routine: fighting but not fighting, dancing but not dancing. A series of feints and ritual attacks, mostly made with the feet, the legs lifted high, the kicks made back-ward, bodies cartwheeling and ducking, never making contact. Karate blows that landed on empty air. The perfor-mance was lithe and elegant, and Faustino couldn't help despising it. In his opinion, it was typical of the so-called "African culture" of the North: empty gestures accompanied by "ethnic" music. Pointless and backward-looking. Mean-while, the streets of San Juan were haunted by ratty children begging for money to feed their mothers' crack habits. That was the real "culture" of the Deep North, and no amount of prancing about to tom-toms was going to fix that.

The two boys left the stage to be replaced by another pair. Faustino returned his gaze to the sea.

A voice from a neighboring table said, *"Paqueira."*

"I know," Faustino said, not looking around.

"From a West African word meaning 'combat.' On the plantations, fighting was forbidden. So the slaves disguised their traditional ways of fighting as dancing. The owners didn't know the difference. Only the slaves knew who were the winners and who were the losers."

Faustino said, "Very interesting." Turning, he saw that the tour guide was no longer wearing his identity tag. His face was bisected vertically by the shadow of the awning. Like an elegant mask, half copper, half ebony. Faustino noticed for the first time that it had an imperfection: the man's lower lip had a kink in it, above a short pale scar. Someone, it seemed, had found his handsomeness irritating and had tried to spoil it.

Edson Bakula smiled. "You find it tedious."

Faustino shrugged. "Have you been following me? To give me another history lesson?"

"No. I usually stop off here between shifts. I live over there." He made a gesture toward nowhere in particular. "May I join you, Señor Faustino?"

Faustino pushed the free chair away from the table with his foot. "Be my guest. So, you know my name?"

"Yes. I read the papers. Some of us can, you know. And I saw you on television being interviewed when El Gato announced his retirement. Very interesting. I got the impression that there were things you chose not to talk about."

Faustino watched the young man's eyes but said nothing.

Bakula smiled again. "No," he said, "you are quite right. None of my business. I apologize."

Faustino forgave him with a gesture.

"I would like to thank you again," the guide said. "For coming to my assistance. For volunteering to be chained."

"It didn't look like anyone else was going to."

"No. People find it a bit embarrassing. For one reason or another. But the Tourism Office insists that we try to do it."

Maybe, Faustino thought. *Or maybe you enjoy it.*

"So, Señor, you are here to investigate Brujito's Sensational Disappearance?" Edson Bakula spoke the phrase as if it were a newspaper headline.

"As a matter of fact, I'm not. I'm . . . on vacation. It's rainy down south at this time of year. I'm here to soak up the sunshine. And the history and the, er, culture, of course."

The guide nodded seriously, as though he had not heard the irony. He tipped a hand toward the building behind them.

"The market was originally the slave hospital, did you know that? Built in 1724. Restored in 1980. It is an official historical monument."

Faustino tried to sound interested. "Hospital? I'm surprised they bothered with that kind of thing."

"It wasn't a hospital in the modern sense of the word. More like the kind of place where you fatten up cattle before they go to market. By the time the slaves got off the ships — he ones that survived the voyage — most were too weak to fetch a decent price. They didn't have the strength to climb up to the city. Most of us had to be carried ashore."

Faustino noted the word *us*. "Yes, a terrible business," he said. Then, in an attempt to change the subject: "May I buy you a drink? Or do you have to be somewhere?"

"No, I have plenty of time. Thank you. A mixed juice, please."

Faustino turned to signal a waitress and found himself looking closely at an impressively muscled torso. It belonged to a great slab of a man holding a collecting tin. He tipped it, and coins slooshed.

"For the *paqueira* display," he said, smiling pleasantly.

Faustino felt in his pocket for change, trying not to sigh.

Faustino saw the new stadium almost half an hour before he reached it. It gleamed above the industrial haze like some intergalactic research craft crouched on the surface of a gaseous planet. When the Estadio Flora signs began, he made a series of hair-raising, horn-blasting maneuvers and got into the inside lane. From the top of the exit, the vastness of the stadium became apparent; it had to be, Faustino thought, at least the size of the Maracanã in Rio or the Nou Camp in Barcelona. And Deportivo San Juan was only a middle-ranking club; where the hell had the money come from to build this place? Gilberto da Silva had deep pockets, but not that deep, surely. Did the old boy wake up in a cold financial sweat at nights? Probably not; the very rich are not like the rest of us. And even if he did, it was probably worth it to keep his wife happy. Faustino now noticed — it made him smile — that it wasn't only the stadium that was named after her; the broad approach road he was now on was the Avenida Flora.

He parked, as he'd been instructed, in the service area, realizing why this had been necessary. A large mob of reporters was gathered at the grandiose front entrance, the loggia. Two TV trucks with satellite dishes on their roofs, radio cars, a snack van doing good business. No, he wouldn't want to shove through that crowd, explaining to his so-called colleagues why he could walk through those pearly gates when they couldn't.

The door had the number 116 on it. Faustino buzzed and then spoke into the intercom. A burly man in a DSJ sweatshirt checked his ID and led him along a narrow corridor, which emerged into the rear of the main reception area. Air-conditioning like a pure mountain breeze. Waiting for the elevator, Faustino enjoyed observing the sweaty pack of press hounds outside the smoked-glass doors. On the third floor, he stood in the deserted VIP lounge, gazing out through its glass wall. The field below him was perfect, a lustrous two-tone carpet of green stripes. In the stand opposite, the black seats among the red formed *DSJ* in vast letters. The retractable roof soared above him, a great glass bat wing with steel sinews.

"My God," he said aloud.

A voice came from behind him: "Yeah. Kinda impressive, isn't it?"

Cesar Fabian, the DSJ trainer, was a well-built, slightly paunchy man in his mid-fifties with cropped gray hair and deep creases in his forehead like cracks in baked earth. His handshake was surprisingly gentle, considering the size of his hands.

"I thought it would be more pleasant to talk here, rather than in the poky hole they call my office." He glanced at the unattended chrome and leather bar. "I guess I could find someone to make us some coffee."

"It's OK," Faustino said. "I'm fine."

The two men settled themselves into sternly modern armchairs. Faustino took his new and very expensive recorder from its case and laid it on the glass-topped table. Scowling at its tiny enigmatic buttons, he said, "You happy to talk to this gizmo, Cesar? Basically, I'm looking for anecdotal stuff. You know, the kind of thing that'll give me a picture of Gato when he first joined DSJ, when he came to live with you and your wife. What it was like having this kid from the jungle land on you."

"Sure," Fabian said. "Mind you, when you first phoned, I assumed you wanted to talk about the Brujito business."

Faustino sighed. "Yeah. It's a hell of a story. I consider it extremely inconsiderate of the young man to pull this stunt while I'm otherwise engaged."

"Is that what you think it is? A stunt?"

Faustino shrugged. "Reading between the lines, that's

what most of my esteemed colleagues seem to think. Are they wrong?"

"Yeah," Fabian said with emphasis. "They're wrong. I'm ninety-nine percent certain of that. The kid doesn't do stunts. Not off the field, anyway. He's not like that."

There was a suppressed heat in Fabian's voice. Faustino sat back from the recorder.

"What *is* he like, Cesar? You know him well?"

"Well enough to know that his disappearance isn't some kinda scam or him having a tantrum. He's a straight up-and-down kid. Quiet, kinda shy. A country boy. No big ego thing about him at all. All the superstar crap in the media hardly touched him."

Faustino raised an eyebrow. "Really? All the girls and the partying and—"

"Garbage," Fabian said, almost angrily. "Absolute bull-shit. Just the tabloids and idiot TV stations doing what they always do. The kid's only just eighteen, for Chrissake. And he's religious."

"Is he? What, devout Catholic, you mean?"

Fabian grunted softly, tilting his head. "Well, you know. That crazy up-country stuff . . . but it kinda blends into regular religion, yeah. Whatever, he's serious about it. Like, before a big game there's this *pai* he needs to talk to—"

"*Pai?*"

"Yeah, you know. Priest, shaman, whatever you wanna call it. Some old guy. It's cool. Most players are superstitious, as you know. Have to put the left cleat on first, can't have anybody whistling in the locker room, that kinda thing. But apart from that, the kid just loves to play. It's all he seems to think about. It's not exactly normal, maybe not even completely healthy, but that's how he is. There's no way he'd be involved in some sort of . . . I dunno."

"OK," Faustino said. "That's pretty much the conclusion I'd come to. So? The cops say it's not a kidnapping, which is the other obvious thing."

Fabian pulled the corners of his mouth down and exhaled through his nose.

"The cops. Well . . . you know, the fact is that in this part of the world, kidnapping's the second most popular sport after soccer. Well, I exaggerate, but not much. It's like you only have to be *this* famous"—he held up his thumb and forefinger, an eighth of an inch apart—"to be kidnapped. Or your husband or your kid or whatever. Last month, some girl who reads the weather on the TV, for Chrissake, had to pay to get her daughter back. You know what? I sometimes worry about my wife. And I'm a nobody."

Faustino made a sympathetic face.

"But," Fabian added, "I'm not convinced it was kidnapping."

"Why not?"

Fabian looked over his shoulder and then down at Faustino's piece of Japanese technology.

"That thing running, Paul?"

"Er . . . no. See the little orange light there? It turns green when it's recording. Why?"

He had no need to ask, really. Obviously the da Silvas had imposed a vow of silence on their staff. That was one reason the newspapers were running on the spot and the gaggle of reporters at DSJ's front door had that look of peasants besieging a rich city. But Cesar Fabian clearly had something to get off his chest. And it was a fairly big chest.

"OK, Cesar. This is off the record. I'm not working on the story anyway. But how come you don't think Brujito was kidnapped?"

"In the first place," Fabian said, "it's gone on too long. These things are usually worked out, one way or another, in three or four days. And no one saw the kid being bundled into a van or anything. Know why? Because he wasn't. He left the ground by the home-team entrance, alone. Two security guys saw him go. So did the CCTV cameras. They also filmed him walking away from the stadium, heading for the pedestrian bridge over the *avenida*."

"Did they? I didn't see that anywhere in the papers."

"Yeah, well. I guess there are things Lord and Lady da Silva want kept quiet."

"Right. Which is why you haven't told me any of this."

"Exactly."

The two men sat in companionable silence for several moments. A maintenance man in a red jumpsuit walked through the lounge. When he had gone, Faustino said, "I'm right in thinking you were on the sideline at that game, aren't I? I mean, I've read the stories, watched the match on TV, but nothing much seemed to happen to the kid. Did you see anything?"

"No, not really. We were all over Atlético from the start, as you know. I mean, it was a game we were certain to win. Atlético should never have got as far as the semifinal in the first place. Morientes, like any good manager, gave our guys a real heavy talking-to before the game about being over-confident, staying tight at the back, all of that. But we were going to win for sure. And when Brujito scored our second, just before halftime, we seemed to have it wrapped up."

"And at halftime," Faustino asked, "in the locker room, Brujito was OK?"

"Sure. Quiet, like he usually is, but happy. It was a lovely goal that he'd scored, and the other players were, you know, ruffling his hair and hugging him and all that stuff. And when the buzzer went, he was straight up on his feet, running in place, couldn't wait to get out for the second half, same as usual. Then, fifteen minutes or so in, he just seemed to lose it."

Faustino said, "The phrase I keep reading in the papers is that the boy 'broke down.' Which usually means the player got some kind of injury out of nowhere, like a hamstring or something. Is that what happened?"

"No. Definitely not. Brujito screwed up the penalty, and everyone on the bench—everyone in the city—was gutted. But there didn't seem to be anything physically wrong with the kid. It's just that he'd stopped playing. Morientes substituted him a couple of minutes later, as you know, and when he came off, I went up to him and put his warm-up jacket around his shoulders and said something like, 'Are you hurting? Are you OK?' and he shook his head. But instead of sitting down on the bench, he went straight off down the tunnel toward the locker room."

"What, like he was pissed off at being substituted?"

"No," Fabian said, "nothing like that. He just seemed sort of . . . dazed. Anyway, Morientes gave me a look, and I sent my assistant, Werner, to check the boy out. He says that when he went into the locker room, Brujito was squatting in a corner, just staring into space. Werner tried to talk to him, said it was like talking to a dummy. 'Vacant' was the word he used. So he left him there and came back to the field."

"And you lost the game."

"Yep," Fabian said. "Four–two. It was like when Brujito was subbed, the heart went out of us. When the final whistle went, it was like all hell broke loose. Plastic bottles, coins, God knows what showering down on us, booing like I'd never heard before. Sounded like about a million animals in an abattoir. We hustled the players off the field fast as we could, and when we got to the locker room, Brujito had vanished. His uniform was in a heap in the corner where Werner had left him. Looked like he'd evaporated out of it. And no one has seen him since."

Faustino rested his chin on his folded hands, thinking. When he looked up, he caught Fabian glancing at his watch.

"Yeah, OK, Cesar. Thanks." He poked experimentally at the recorder and the minuscule light turned green.

"So then, the business at hand. El Gato."

"Gato, yeah. Jeez, I tell you what, Paul: I wish we had him now." Fabian aimed a thumb up at the stadium roof. "Gilberto da Silva spent twenty million on that thing, to keep the rain off. He shoulda spent it on players. Our defense leaks like a damn sieve. Which reminds me."

He reached into a pocket and took out a long slim envelope. "Present for you. Two tickets for Sunday's game. Directors' box. We're playing Espirito Santo, so at least there'll be one decent team on the field."

The air-conditioning in the rental car wasn't up to the job, and when Faustino got to his hotel, he went up to his room, stripped to his underwear, and stood akimbo in front of the AC unit for several minutes. Then he sat on the bed and began to play back his conversation with Cesar Fabian about El Gato. After ninety seconds, he turned the machine off and stared at the far wall for a while. Then he reached for his phone. Maximo Salez's answering machine gave a cell phone number. At the third attempt, Faustino got a response from it.

"Yeah?"

"Maximo? This is Paul Faustino."

"My God! Maestro! What have I done to deserve this honor?"

"You tell me. Max, listen. I want to talk to you. Where are you?"

"Er, I'm in a meeting at the moment, but . . ."

Yes, Faustino thought, *a meeting between your mouth and a beer.* The background to Salez's voice was other voices and sleazy music.

"OK, so how about an hour from now? I'll come to the office."

"What? You mean you're in San Juan?"

"I'm afraid so. And, Max, do you have a video of the DSJ-Atlético semifinal? I'd like to watch it."

Maximo Salez was a thin, nervy man with poor skin and a taste for loud shirts. His writing was, usually, a mechanical recitation of jargon and clichés, but every now and again it would erupt, like a tropical flower after rain, into drunkenly poetic passages of description, which *La Nación's* sports editor would ruthlessly delete. He greeted Faustino with an ironic bow that failed to conceal his anxiety.

"Excuse the mess in here," he said. "Things are a little hectic right now. Pull that chair over."

His office was a miserable little hutch separated from the reception area by a glass wall. Salez clattered the venetian blind closed, and the light turned gray. He sat himself down on a swivel chair that had seen better days and supported better men.

"Well, Paul. This is an unexpected treat. I didn't know you were here in the Deep North. I thought you were on leave."

Faustino took his time lighting a cigarette. When he considered that Salez had suffered enough, he said, "I am. Relax, Maximo. You look like you've got hemorrhoids. I haven't come up here to take over the Brujito story."

"Ah. Well, naturally I thought—"

"Although, of course, I *am* interested."

"Right," Salez said. "Of course. It's a helluva thing. If you've got any thoughts—"

"I read your piece in yesterday's edition. You seemed to buy the kidnapping story."

"Well—"

"And within hours of your filing the piece, the police dismissed it as a hoax. At a news conference."

"Listen, that don't mean a thing. I mean, if the boy *has* been kidnapped, the cops *would* deny it, wouldn't they? They wouldn't want us all over them like a rash while they were negotiating or whatever. Besides, Paul, you can't believe a word the police say, not in this city. They're all as bent as a dog's back leg. Believe me, I know."

Faustino's expression did not suggest that he believed anything. Or anyone. Especially Max Salez.

"What about the idea that the kid had some sort of nervous breakdown, couldn't take the pressure, maybe?"

Salez stuck his bottom lip out and shook his head. "Nah. I don't buy it. Seems to me he doesn't *have* any nerves. Either that or he's too dumb to know where they are. Hard to tell which."

Faustino reflected, not for the first time, that stupidity and complacency were a very unpleasing combination. Especially in a so-called journalist.

"So you're stuck with the kidnapping theory."

"Well, hey, I'm not *stuck* with it, Paul. I mean, young Señor de Barros is a very valuable piece of property. You know what DSJ paid for him? When he was sixteen years old? Nothing. A signing-on fee. Enough for a month's supply of candy. And what d'you reckon he's worth now? Ten million? Fifteen? If he was for sale, of course. Which as far as I know he isn't."

Faustino nodded slowly, as if Salez had just shared a rare and important snippet of information. He stubbed his cigarette out in an overflowing ashtray. While doing so, he said, "Did you know that Brujito left the ground unaccompanied? That he just walked out of the home-team entrance like he normally would?"

Salez blinked. "Who says?"

"A reliable source."

"Right," Salez said, and clammed up.

"You know what, Maximo? You're a very lucky man. I'd part with a few teeth to be covering a story like this. I'd be out on the street chasing up every lowlife I knew who might have heard even half a whisper."

"Well, Jesus, Paul, what d'you think I've been doing? That's what we've all been doing. Man, there isn't a single scumbag in this city we haven't waved our wallets at."

"And?"

"*Nada*. Nothing."

Faustino thought about that. "I assume, then, the conclusion you've come to is that if, *if* this is a kidnapping, then it's not the usual suspects. That right?"

Maximo Salez picked up a ballpoint pen and examined it as if it were the first one he'd ever seen.

"Yeah," he said eventually. "I guess so. Maybe."

Faustino watched the other man's face for a couple of seconds. Then he said, "Let's watch the video."

The TV room contained a small collection of soft and mangy chairs. The window ledge was lined with empty plastic bottles and beer cans.

Faustino said, "Let's skip to the second half."

The cameras had lingered on Brujito, even at times when he was not involved in the play. He was not—as certain magazines liked to point out—a particularly handsome youth, and he held his head lowered slightly, like a solemn but dangerous dog. He was short, for a player, with a rather heavy upper body. The same sort of build as Maradona or the young English forward Rooney, the build that gives you a low center of gravity, making it hard for defenders to knock you off balance. He was the kind of boy that, if you saw him in the street, you would take to be slow-witted and slow-moving. And when he had played his first games for DSJ, opposing players had made the same mistake and paid dearly for it.

Watching the screen, Faustino was again astonished by Brujito's ability to switch from a standstill to incredible speed without, apparently, any intervening period of acceleration. It was simply that at one moment he was strolling and the next he was at full power. Yes, he had a repertoire of skills and tricks that no boy of his age was entitled to, but Faustino understood that it was this extraordinary variation in pace that was the key to his game. In particular, he would brake suddenly, as if he had run out of ideas, or space. Got stuck. He would not look up, not seek support. It would tempt defenders to close in. It would distort their formation. Then, with what looked like nothing more than a shrug, a shuffle of feet, a sidestep, the ball would be gone. And so would he. There was, Faustino thought, something slightly spooky about it. Because even on replay you couldn't see what he'd done. What you could see, though, was that whenever he received the ball, a ripple of panic spread through the Atlético defense.

But, as Cesar Fabian had said, early in the second half the boy seemed to lose the plot. He flubbed a number of simple passes. Twice in less than five minutes, he was caught offside, stranded like a crab at low tide. A minute later, Cabral, the Atlético defender given the dread responsibility of guarding the boy, took the ball from him with a halfhearted tackle. The camera caught Cabral looking over his shoulder as though he'd done something clever without knowing how.

71

"Weird, wouldn't you say?" Salez said.

"Interesting," Faustino said.

When Vadinho, the DSJ wing, was chopped down in the Atlético penalty area, Salez pressed the *pause* button on the remote.

"Now, watch this," he said. "Brujito has been crap for some time. I was at the game, OK, and I know that Morientes was ready to substitute him. He'd got Berger warming up on the sideline. Brujito must have known he was going to be taken out. Then there's this penalty."

Salez hit *play*.

"Vadinho wants to take it himself, see? He carries the ball to the spot. But then Brujito comes up to him, and they have this discussion. It's obvious Brujito wants to take it. It's also obvious Vadinho doesn't want him to. I think that Vadinho thought Brujito was injured. We all did. Morientes did. It's not on the video, but he was going ape from the bench. But Brujito takes no notice. He insists on taking the penalty."

"Which he was entitled to. He'd taken the last, what, four for DSJ? And left the goalkeeper for dead in every one."

"Yeah, Paul, but the point is that Brujito had lost it. Look at him. He looks . . . I dunno, depressed or something. So why does he want to take the kick? And, here we go, it's got to be the saddest attempt I've ever seen. The keeper just takes it out of the air and says, 'Thank you very much.'"

Faustino watched the Atlético supporters jeering and celebrating, then watched Brujito walk to the bench to be substituted. Humiliated.

"Max, rewind the tape, please. There's a bit where Brujito is out on the left wing near the corner flag and Cabral is closing him down. Ten minutes before the penalty, something like that. No, not there. Forward. Now back a bit. Yes, here."

Brujito had taken the ball down the left sideline, dangerously close to the corner flag. Cabral was crowding him, watching the ball, shielding it against the cross. Because from this position all Brujito could do was cross. Another Athlético defender had moved into the frame to cut off any move Brujito might try to make toward the center. And Faustino understood that this was exactly what Brujito wanted: to draw another defender toward him. Because it left a gap into which a DSJ midfielder could run. And when that space opened, Brujito would, somehow, by some outrageous magic, get the ball into it, as he had done many times before. But he didn't. Cabral slid in, won the ball, and cleared it upfield.

"Go back again," Faustino said, dragging his chair closer to the TV.

Salez rewound the tape, little bursts of reverse action.

"What? Here?"

"Yeah," Faustino said, squinting. "Hold it there."

Brujito had the ball against the inside of his left foot. He was a couple of paces from the corner flag, hemmed in by Cabral, who was spreading his arms like a man trying to shepherd an unpredictable animal. The other Atlético defender was just coming into the shot from the left. But what interested Faustino was that Brujito was not looking at either of them. Nor was he looking at the ball. At that vital instant, he seemed to be staring into the crowd, as if he had just been struck by something thrown at him and was wondering where it had come from.

"Paul? What?"

Faustino lifted a hand. "Wait."

He studied the screen. Behind Brujito the electronic advertising board was displaying a word fragment, the letters *esp*. Beyond it, in the space reserved for wheelchair users, were parked a heavy man wrapped in a DSJ flag and an openmouthed boy clutching the arms of his chair; standing behind them was an oldish guy all in white—a medical person, perhaps. The rest of the image was a living mosaic of red and black. Red-and-black shirts, scarves, banners. Faces painted in red and black stripes, red and black quarters. Heads tiny beneath red-and-black wigs. Masks. Like a congregation of witch doctors. And Brujito was looking somewhere into this mass. But at what?

Salez pressed the *play* button.

Cabral wins the ball and makes his hasty escape, but Brujito stays frozen, still looking away. Then the camera goes chasing the action, and the moment is over.

74

◆　◆　◆

Faustino was back in his car with the key in the ignition when he felt that familiar itch, almost a prickle, at the base of his brain. His onboard lie detector had a message for him. Something wasn't right.

He ran through the adjectives that one could apply to Max Salez: *lazy, sad, seedy, unattractive, envious, provincial.* A fool. But even fools sometimes know things that other people don't. So how about *shifty, evasive, defensive, secretive?* Yes, that was more like the Salez he had spent the last hour and a half with. The way he'd fiddled with that pen, saying, "I guess so. Maybe." Not *embarrassed.* Not *inadequate.* No, the sneaky little bastard *knew* something.

From where he was parked, Faustino did not have a good view of the building he had just left, and the entrance was continually obscured by people coming and going from the fast-food joint next door. Damn! Still, he sat, sweltering, for ten minutes and finally he was rewarded. There was Salez: no mistaking that horrible lime-green-and-orange shirt. Faustino put his sunglasses on. He started the car, and when Salez got into a yellow taxi, Faustino pulled away from the curb and followed it, keeping two cars between himself and the cab.

Ten minutes later, it stopped in a nondescript square called Plaza Bandiera. Faustino passed the cab and parked, illegally, fifty yards ahead and on the opposite side. When the cab drove off, Salez walked a mere five paces to the window of a kitchenware shop and took an unlikely interest in the goods on display. Except that every few seconds, he turned to scan the traffic. Faustino rummaged in his jacket pocket for his cigarettes, but before he could light one, a police car—a blue-and-white sedan with the SJDP insignia—pulled up alongside the shop. Salez strolled, as casually as he could manage, to the front passenger window and leaned his head in. After a brief conversation, he straightened up and looked around him. He appeared hesitant, undecided. Then, seemingly in response to something the driver said, he opened the rear passenger door and got in. The car moved off. It turned right and right again at the top of the square and came past Faustino. The driver was white, or nearly so, and not in uniform.

Faustino was not at all happy about tailing a cruiser belonging to the notorious San Juan Department of Police, so he was relieved when he lost it at the complex traffic lights on Avenida San Pedro. He swore and thumped the steering wheel, of course, but he was relieved. Until he realized that he didn't know how to get back to his hotel, that the light had changed, and that the traffic backed up behind him was blaring a fanfare from hell.

By the end of the week, Paul Faustino had come to like the slow ritualistic breakfast that was a feature of his hotel and (for the more privileged) life in the Deep North generally. In his real world, there was no way he would have started the day with fresh fruit juice and then embarked on a five-course meal that involved both scrambled eggs and chocolate cake. But then, in his real world, there was no such thing as breakfast; when you worked up to the wire, the one-in-the-morning deadline, and then hit the bars, lunch was the first meal that you took. Or refused. Up here, though, the rhythm was different. Stoke up with calories early in the day, then eke them out, moving slowly through the heat and the humidity. Watch your step on the harshly cobbled streets, the tilted pavements.

Northern lethargy had gripped him gently. There was no reason, really, to stay on in San Juan. He'd gotten most of what he wanted, been where he needed to go, taken several pictures with his (almost) idiot-proof camera. He'd dined with the Fabians, and Ana Fabian had turned out to be both a fine cook and a rich source of human interest stories about the young El Gato. He'd had a few very expensive drinks with Milton Acuna, former director of soccer at DSJ and now a TV commentator. He'd had an informative, if difficult, lunch—the man had cancer—with Pablo Laval, the DSJ keeper whom Gato had displaced. It was disappointing that he had not managed to swing an interview with Flora da Silva. Understandable, considering the circumstances, but disappointing nonetheless. Some other time, perhaps, when she was not busy negotiating with kidnappers. If that was what she was doing.

According to the press and TV, there had been no further developments in the Brujito story. Faustino found this both intriguing and frustrating. And slightly offensive— journalists shouldn't be satisfied with nothing. *He* wouldn't be, if he were on the story. But he wasn't. All the same, it struck him as lazy and pathetic that the best today's edition of *El Norte* could manage was a smeary snapshot of the da Silvas in the back of a chauffeur-driven car under the headline FLORA AND GILBERTO: THE AGONY CONTINUES. And no story. He was half tempted to ring the editor and give him a piece of his mind. To disturb his peace of mind. There was nothing in *La Nación* either. Salez appeared to have gone quiet, or maybe he'd sent in chunks of empty verbiage that Vittorio on the news desk had spiked.

There was the DSJ–Espirito Santo game tomorrow, of course. Probably without the lovely Flora da Silva to gaze at during the slow moments, and almost certainly no way of talking to her even if she was there. So he ought to pack, check out, drop the rental car at the airport, fly home. Nevertheless, he went back to the buffet table, poured himself more coffee, and put another slice of cake onto his plate. He was about to sit down again when his phone burbled. He flipped it open; the caller ID showed CROCODILE.

He pressed the green button. "Carmen. What a delightful surprise. How are you? Are you missing me?"

The voice in his ear said, "What are you doing at this moment?"

Faustino's boss was not famous for her small talk. He carried her out of the dining room into the patio garden, where improbable flowers rioted in the shade.

"I'm just finishing breakfast."

"At nine thirty?"

Damn the woman. "Life runs on a different timetable up here, Carmen."

"So it seems. Did you watch your local news this morning?"

"Nope. Should I have?"

"A body was fished out of the docks. The docks at San Juan."

"I don't suppose that's an unusual occurrence."

"It was Maximo Salez."

It seemed to Faustino that the flowers surrounding him trembled in a breeze he couldn't feel. He leaned against the wall.

"Paul? Did you hear me?"

"Yeah, Carmen, I heard you. Thanks for breaking it to me so gently. How do you know it was Salez?"

"His wallet was still in his pocket. We had a call from the San Juan police a short time ago."

"Christ."

"Listen, Paul. I'm flying someone up there later. But I need something for this evening's edition. I want you to get over to the San Juan police HQ and —"

"Carmen, Carmen. I'm on *leave*."

"From work, Paul, not from life. You knew the guy."

"Yeah, he was a jerk."

"Yes," Carmen d'Andrade said. "But he was one of our jerks."

It was a new building, but the textured concrete was already streaked with something that looked like soot, that universal feature of San Juan's architecture. There were three officers at the duty desk. Faustino chose to approach the female one, which was probably a mistake.

"I'd like to speak to the officer leading the investigation into the death of Maximo Salez."

She looked away from her computer screen eventually.

"I bet you would," she said.

"I am — was, I should say — a colleague of Señor Salez."

"You are a reporter." It wasn't a question.

"Yes, but . . ."

She switched her stare back to her screen. "There will be a statement to the press later this morning. If you wish to wait, you may join your other 'colleagues' over there."

Without looking, she gestured toward a glass partition at the far end of the lobby. Beyond it, a small group of bored men and women sat inside a cloud of cigarette smoke.

Faustino held his ground for half a minute, but the policewoman refused to look at him. He moved a short distance along the counter and stood there, thinking, drumming his fingers. Then he sighed and took one of his business cards from his inside pocket, along with the envelope that Cesar Fabian had given him. He wrote a few words on the back of the card and put it into the envelope with the tickets, aware that the woman was watching him out of the corner of her eye. He sealed the envelope, then reached over and dropped it onto her keyboard.

"Señora," he said quietly, "I am here to give information, not gather information. I think it would be a good idea if you gave this to an investigating officer now. I'll wait for ten minutes. If no one wants to speak to me, I shall leave at the end of that time."

Seven minutes later, Faustino was shown into an office

spookily similar to that of the late Maximo Salez, except for the pistol in its shoulder holster slung over the back of the chair behind the desk. The athletic-looking black man with his head shaved smooth as a bowling ball introduced himself as Sergeant Artur Fillol. Faustino's business card was lying on the desk next to the white envelope.

"Pleasure to meet you, Señor Faustino. Please, take a seat. I like the stuff you write in the papers. But I haven't seen anything by you recently."

"Thank you. And no, I'm taking a break."

Fillol nodded. "So you're not here in a, uh, professional capacity. You haven't taken up crime reporting instead."

"Not really."

Fillol's smile didn't flicker but his eyebrows went up. "Not *really*?"

"Well, of course I'd like to know what happened to poor Max. And so would my editor. Max's editor."

The sergeant leaned forward and tweaked the soccer tickets halfway out of the envelope.

"And you thought these might help you find out before the rest of that mob out there?"

"Oh, the tickets. I completely forgot they were in there. Should be a decent game, don't you think?"

Fillol sat back and regarded Faustino gravely. "How well did you know Salez? Were you friends with the guy?"

"No. I didn't much like him, to tell the truth."

"Nor did I," Fillol said. "When'd you last see him?"

"Um, three days ago. The, er, fourteenth. At his office. We were discussing the Brujito thing."

"Yeah," Fillol said. "What time was this? What time did you leave?"

Before Faustino could answer, a voice from the doorway behind him said, "Artur? How long before you're through here?"

The sergeant shrugged. "Not very long, I guess."

The other man came into the room, past Faustino, not looking at him, saying, "I want to talk to everyone in fifteen minutes, upstairs. Have a look at these before you come."

He dropped a file with yellow plastic covers onto Fillol's desk. Then he did look over at Faustino and switched a smile on. "Excuse the interruption, Señor."

The SJDP tag clipped to his lapel identified him as Captain Eduardo Varga. Faustino experienced a lurch of recognition. He'd seen the man before. Driving a blue-and-white cruiser. Which was not something you'd expect a senior detective to be doing.

"No problem," Faustino said generously.

When Varga had gone, Sergeant Fillol couldn't resist having a peek at the file, and Faustino couldn't help seeing the uppermost photograph.

"Dear God," he said. "Is that Maximo?"

Fillol considered the question, then got up and closed the door that Varga had left open. He sat back down and slid the picture across the desk.

Salez looked deader than anyone had a right to. His arms and legs were unrealistically thin under the saturated clothes. The hair clung like seaweed to the gray face, and the mouth was open; the fillings in his teeth were clearly visible. And some awful thing protruded from the front of the gaudy shirt.

Faustino felt his stomach shift, and his mouth filled with saliva. "He was stabbed?" he asked stupidly.

"That's the theory we're working on. The knife embedded in the chest seems to indicate something like that."

Fillol slid two more photos toward Faustino. "This is the weapon. Seen anything like it before?"

The blade was wide and curved symmetrically to a point, like a leaf. The handle — wood, or maybe bone — was carved into the shape of two figures back to back. Outsize heads, or perhaps masks, with gashes for mouths: one smiling, one grieving. Crescent slits representing closed eyes. Each figure held what looked like some kind of staff with an ax head at the end of it.

"It's a sacrificial knife," Fillol said. "Used in certain *Veneración* ceremonies. You know Veneration, Worship? Ancestor Worship?"

"I know a bit about it," Faustino murmured, still sickeningly preoccupied by the thought of having a thing like that thrust into one's body.

"Not the ideal stabbing weapon," Fillol [...] you'd want something narrower and a bit long[...] victims of this kind of weapon are chickens or g[...] carving is meant to be Maco. He is the ancestor who [...] penses law and justice. And revenge."

Faustino looked up at him.

Fillol smiled thinly. "No, I'm not an expert. I only know it's Maco because we use him on our crime posters, in a useless attempt to persuade people that we have powers we don't really have. Did Salez talk about Veneration at all? Could he have been mixed up in that sort of thing? Working on a story about it, something like that?"

"No. He didn't mention it at all. I can't imagine he could've been involved . . . I mean, he's not even, wasn't even . . ."

Fillol cocked his head. "Not even what? Black? Of African descent? It's not unknown for non-blacks to get into Veneration. Besides, everyone up here is African one way or another."

Faustino shoved the pictures away. "So you believe this was some sort of religious killing?"

"I don't believe anything," Fillol said. "But whoever did it left the knife in. They wanted us to find it." He glanced at his watch. "So, what time did you say you left Salez's office?"

"Four, maybe a couple of minutes after."

"And you didn't see him again after that?"

Faustino knew a can of worms when he saw one. He

nd said, "No. That was the last
astard."

that the interview was over,
ne detective's hand, and turned to go.
You forgot these."

ding out the envelope with the tickets in it.
ustino took them. He noted a certain cold
it in the sergeant's eyes.

Fillol said, "You'd met Captain Varga before?"

"Who?"

"The officer who came in earlier. It seemed to me that you recognized him."

Faustino frowned thoughtfully, then shook his head. "No."

"Sure?"

"Yes, quite sure. I know hardly anyone in San Juan. And this is certainly the first time I've had the pleasure of meeting any of its police officers."

Fillol nodded. "Very well." He took a card from his pocket. "If you think of anything else or want to contact me, use the second of these two numbers. Please speak only to me personally, OK? And don't leave any messages on the answering machine."

Fillol's smile did not change the look in his eyes.

"Our message service here is not always reliable."

From his hotel room, Faustino phoned his piece to the news desk of *La Nación*, with strict instructions that his name should not appear above it or in it. Then he changed into a fresh shirt and walked down to the Old Quarter, tacking back and forth across the narrowing streets to stay in the shade. There were few people and little traffic in The Pillory at this time of day; the heat was so intense that it seemed to resonate in the air like the echo of a gong. At the corner of the Calle Libertador, he found a small café and dived into the shadow of its awning, gasping. He sat sipping iced coffee, keeping watch on the small door cut into the massive main entrance to the Church of Christ the Redeemer.

After twenty minutes had passed, Faustino began to wonder if he'd gotten his timing wrong. He hadn't. A small group of tourists emerged from the church, hastily rummaging in their bags and pockets for sunglasses. He watched them shake hands with their guide, tip him, then disperse, hassled by two small boys bearing sheets of cardboard to which strings of beads were pinned.

Faustino stood and stepped into the pitiless light. But there was no need for him to cross the street; Edson Bakula saw him immediately. Faustino raised his hand, then mimed drinking.

Bakula stared, motionless, for several seconds, then approached.

"I'd like to buy you a drink," Faustino said. "If you've nothing better to do."

"Sure. Why not?"

When the waiter appeared, Bakula ordered a rum-and-lime cocktail, speaking in the peculiar lilting accent of the North. It was not the voice he used in his trade, the one he now used to address Faustino.

"So, Señor Faustino."

"Paul, please."

"OK, *Paul*."

"I'd like to talk to you about Veneration," Faustino said.

"Ah. Well, there is an excellent museum up on—"

"Been there, done that. I've also been to a Veneration, er, ceremony, ritual, whatever the word is. Last time I was here. Six years ago."

"Really. And what did you make of it?"

Indeed, what *had* he made of it?

Faustino had gone with a temporary girlfriend, the two of them squeezed one night into a minibus with a dozen other paying adventurers and driven to one of the outer darknesses of San Juan. They'd sat, shoeless, along three sides of a large, harshly lit shed with whitewashed walls. Against the other wall, four listless-looking drummers sat behind a low altar—a coffee table—upon which were dishes of bread, salt and fruit, and a pile of loosely rolled cigars. Also half a dozen figurines; they'd looked to Faustino like gaudily dressed dolls from a cheap toy store. The twenty or so worshippers were all female, all dressed in white, slavery-era costumes. They milled about in an apparently aimless fashion, ignoring the visitors; now and again they would embrace one another and utter eerie cries like tree-canopy birds.

After a considerable amount of time, the *pai* entered the room. He was a tall light-skinned black man wearing white clothes and a fixed sneer, as though his mustache was giving off a foul smell. He blew long jets of cigar smoke from his flared nostrils. The drummers struck up, and the women began a shuffling, swaying dance, stomping the floor with bare feet. Soon—too soon, Faustino thought—one of them was writhing on the floor in front of the altar, moaning and gabbling in an invented or lost language, while the *pai* blew his smoke over her body and the other women yelped their bird calls.

When this had gone on for several minutes, the possessed woman got to her knees, pressed the *pai*'s hand to the crown of her head, lit a cigar from the altar, and rejoined her companions. Then the whole damned thing had started over again: the drumming, the dancing, another woman possessed, the room filling with shifting strata of blue smoke.

At the beginning of the evening, Faustino had felt a bit . . . embarrassed, perhaps. Even intimidated. After two hours of this repetitive mumbo jumbo, these feelings had given way to a sullen boredom. He and the girl had tried to slip away in search of a taxi, but had found the iron gate between the yard and the street locked. It had been three o'clock in the morning before they'd been delivered back to their hotel. It was odd, really, that such a tedious and irritating experience should have lodged so vividly in his memory. Maybe it was because the two tickets for the performance had cost him eighty dollars.

He said to Edson Bakula, "With all due respect, I think I got screwed."

Bakula smiled happily. "Because they took your hard-earned money off you? Well, yes, of course. But I'm sure you'll be comforted to know that it would have been put to good use. Houses of Worship use their takings from tourists to provide education and medicines for the poor, among other things."

"That's all right, then," Faustino said, lighting a cigarette.

"I take it you were at a white ceremony. White room, white clothes, and so on?"

"Yeah."

"White ceremonies are healing ceremonies. Through the *pai,* people speak with their spirit ancestor, who gives them advice, comfort, strength. And God knows they need it. These people have hard lives."

There was something about Edson Bakula that was . . . what? Patronizing? Schoolmasterish? Something that didn't quite fit with his fine face, his easy smile.

But Faustino nodded understandingly. "And white ceremonies are the ones that tourists get to see, I assume. But there are other kinds?"

Bakula swirled his glass, apparently interested in the way the chunks of lime lurched among the ice.

"In San Juan," he said, "white ceremonies are the most common. This is because for a long time now, people have come here from the country thinking that the life will be easier. It is not. Instead we found hardships, temptations, crimes we had not imagined. And were not ready for. So, of course, the Veneration houses that offered healing became popular. Important."

As a journalist, Paul Faustino was always hugely pleased, as if he'd won a game of cards with a weak hand, when someone avoided answering a question. Because it had been, obviously, a good question. The trick was to wait awhile before asking it again.

So he said, "I noticed that you said 'we' just now. You said *we* found hardships and whatever. So you're not a city boy? You're from the country?"

Edson Bakula raised his hands and leaned back in his chair, smiling. "Ah. You have seen through my cool urban disguise. Yes, of course. I'm from the Cane Country. They still call it that, even though the sugar business collapsed a long, long time ago. You've heard of it?"

"Sure. They also used to call it the Land of the Colonels, is that right? Because plantation owners liked to pretend they were military commanders?"

Bakula emptied his glass and put it down on the table. His smile was a thing of the past.

"Sugar," he said. "Such a soft word. Such a good word for something full of sweetness. Something so *white*, when it is refined."

Faustino concealed a sigh inside a stream of cigarette smoke.

"In fact," Bakula continued, "the Cane Country is a place where a slow holocaust took place. At a low estimate, one million slaves died producing sugar for the colonels. Sugarcane also destroyed the forests and exhausted the soil. So even after slavery was abolished, people continued to die in huge numbers, of poverty, hunger, disease. And alcoholism, of course."

Faustino tapped Bakula's glass with a fingernail.

"Another?" he asked innocently. "I wouldn't mind trying one of those myself."

When the waiter had come and gone, Faustino said, "It's still pretty rough up there in the Cane Country, isn't it? Cheers, by the way."

Edson Bakula hesitated briefly, then clinked his glass against Faustino's. He said, "You could take a taxi to San Juan's new multimillion-dollar airport and in less than an hour be flying over what looks like one of the most desperate parts of Africa. You probably wouldn't believe it."

"And would I be right in thinking," Faustino said, getting there at last, "that up there Veneration isn't all nice touristy white ceremonies dedicated to the healing ancestors like Amalu and Ochandja? That other ancestors have a little more, er, influence? Like Maco, for instance?"

Bakula sat back and studied Faustino's face for several moments. Eventually he said, "Yes, perhaps. So tell me, Señor Faustino — Paul — what is the nature of your interest in these matters? Are you writing something?"

"No."

"Ah." Bakula smiled ironically. "So it's a personal interest? A spiritual quest?"

"Hah!"

"No? You have no interest in spiritual matters?"

"No, thank God," Faustino said. "Fortunately, the

religious gene in my family seems to have skipped a generation. My mother suffered badly from it. I am, happily, a sensualist. The real world is quite enough for me."

"Some would describe such an attitude as superficial."

"Oh yes," Faustino agreed. "I am undeniably a superficial person. I like the surfaces of things. I have yet to see a car that looks better without its paintwork, or a woman who looks better without her skin. Have you?"

Edson Bakula seemed to consider the question seriously. But he said, "So why are we having this conversation?"

Faustino sipped his drink. Then he told Bakula about Maximo Salez and about the knife. The guide listened without interrupting, staring at the surface of the table, running the backs of his fingers through the moisture on the outside of his glass.

When Faustino had finished, Bakula said, "And you imagined that I might be able to cast some light on this business? That I have, what, inside information about the cults in this city?"

Faustino lifted his shoulders, a defensive gesture. "I didn't have anyone else to discuss it with. And you seem like a very well-informed person."

"And I am from the heartland of Maco worship."

"Well, yes, although I didn't know that until . . ."

Bakula looked up at Faustino now. "I can't help you," he said.

"Can't, or won't?"

94

The guide's expression hardly changed, but it was clear that he wasn't used to being challenged. He ran a finger over his disfigured lower lip, then said, "I dare say there have been white people killed in the name of Maco. Considering the history of this place, it would not be surprising. But the knife means nothing in itself. You can buy them in tourist shops, I'm sorry to say."

He stood up.

"Right," Faustino said. "Well, thanks for your time."

"Thank you for the drinks." Bakula looked out at the sun-hammered square. "Perhaps your friend just happened to be in the wrong place at the wrong time. In San Juan most people are."

Wearing only boxer shorts and a T-shirt, Faustino took a beer from the minibar and went out onto his balcony. The lowering sun had filled the street below with shadow but also cruelly illuminated the scabby masonry and skewed roof tiles of the buildings opposite. He watched a plane cross the bay on its low approach to the airport; its fuselage reflected pink light.

On its website, the hotel had made a big deal of the views of the bay that could be enjoyed from the upper floors. In reality, the great swath of blue was interrupted in several places by tall and astonishingly ugly buildings, most of them rearing up from the industrial stretch of the waterfront. Closer to the hotel, perhaps only a street away, the elaborate and crumbling twin campaniles of a church jutted into the sky. Skinny weeds sprouted among their cracked tiles, and Faustino wondered idly how they lived, so far from soil. One of the towers still had its bell, dimly visible inside the arched opening. Inside the other arch, there was only darkness; but as Faustino watched, this darkness changed shape and moved. A humped form moved briefly into the light and became a vulture. It eased its shoulders and stretched its neck like a priest who has sat too long in the confessional; then it turned, crapped, and shuffled back into the shadows.

Faustino finished his beer, then went inside and took a long shower. When he returned to the balcony, the Church of the Vulture was a silhouette against a dirty sky smudged with stars. From somewhere, the lilt of reggae and a whiff of sewage. From the street below, voices and laughter. He lit a cigarette and looked down.

A game of soccer was in progress under the sour yellow light of the streetlamps. Twenty kids, maybe, and a handful of smashed-looking adult spectators squatting with their backs against the wall, sharing beers and joints. One of the players was a skinny kid with his hair shaved close to his scalp, and he was taking the whole thing very seriously. His voice rose above the others, rose all the way to Faustino.

"*Cross!*" he yelled. "*Jesus, man! Why dincha cross? I was open, man!*"

And then he was off again, hurtling back into the dimness between one lamp and the next, ferocious in his pursuit of a much bigger boy.

There were, Faustino concluded, two ways of looking at what had happened to Max Salez.

One: he had been brutally assassinated while doing what good journalists—proper journalists—should be doing: fearlessly shining the flickering light of truth into the dark corners where the rats of criminality lurked and scrabbled. Two: he was a clueless klutz who'd gotten too close to the action and paid the price for it. But in fact it didn't really make much difference which view you took. Because no matter what the sad bastard had been doing, he hadn't deserved to get dumped into the liquid filth of San Juan's harbor with a goat-slitter shoved into his vital organs. Faustino surprised himself by feeling something like righteous indignation. People ought not to be able to murder journalists and get away with it. It wasn't like they were dope dealers or pimps.

So what should he, Faustino, do? Well, clearly he should stick it out in San Juan, try to ensure that Max's murder wasn't conveniently buried in some police file and forgotten. He owed the poor fool that much. (And on the subject of burying, who in God's name would put Max in the ground? Who would be at the funeral? Who would *organize* the funeral? It was somehow hard to imagine that he had parents, brothers, sisters, friends. Faustino hurriedly retreated from this line of thought.)

Then there was the Brujito story. Such a *good* story—and there it was, dangling right in front of Faustino's nose.

It should be taken, written, finished. As a fitting epitaph for Maximo Salez, as much as anything else. What's more, Max's death — if it was connected with the case — made it even better. And despite what that shifty so-and-so Bakula had said, Faustino was pretty sure there *was* a connection. Max had known something, something he hadn't wanted to tell Faustino. Something he'd gotten from the cops, presumably, and following it up had earned him a knife in the chest.

Yes, there were good reasons for staying in San Juan. The cowardly alternative was to scuttle for safety, to get the hell out while he was still in one piece.

There was no real choice.

He went inside and called the airport. There was a two forty-five flight the following afternoon. He booked himself on it, then closed the doors onto the balcony. The last thing he heard was a mixed chorus of jeers and cheers, and the skinny kid shouting, *"Aw, man! It was there for the taking! The hell were you doing?"*

Faustino got dressed and went downstairs. At reception he asked the girl to make up his bill ready for the morning. Then he walked the two blocks to the main road, where he hailed a taxi and told the driver to drop him off at a place on North Beach called Jaquito's. There he ate the seafood special, which was ordinary, and drank too much. He developed a sudden need for company, and as a result had a blurry misunderstanding with a Spanish-looking guy whose girlfriend he'd been chatting up at the bar. For some reason, the cabbie who drove him back to the hotel just before midnight announced that he'd been an alcoholic until he'd been embraced by the irresistible love of Our Lord Jesus Christ. He gave Faustino a business card that showed a taxi driving toward a vast crucifix that radiated beams like a lighthouse. In return, Faustino gave him the smallest tip in the history of cabbying.

When he'd gotten the door to his room open, Faustino's foot skidded on something that lay on the polished veneer floor. Cursing, he reached out to steady himself and by chance his hand landed on the main light switch.

The thing that had almost put him on his back was an envelope. Both it and the single sheet of paper inside were printed with the name of the hotel. The note read:

Meet me in the cathedral at 10 a.m. — *E. Bakula*

THREE: BLESSING

I didn't go to the cane fields. I was put to work in the sugar mill, in the crushing yard. Unloading the cane from the ox wagons, feeding it to the presses, cleaning the runnels the juice ran down, fetching the mush over to the rum house. I kept quiet. I watched. I learned. I didn't let myself die inside, like some of the others. The ones who had gone ghost. I built a shrine in my head. My father was in there, making a cup of his hands for his own blood. The faces from the death ship were in there, and the bodies rolling in the sea like logs. Abela was in there. And the walls and the roof of the shrine were the teachings of the *pai*.

The boss of the mill was an old man with one eye that was blind and milky. He liked me for my steadiness. He had been born on the plantation and knew the white man's language, which he taught me. He also told me about the white men's Worship, about their god who was murdered.

He thought that was why they loved death so much and took it with them everywhere.

In the three years I was in the mill, I saw Colonel d'Oliviera no more than six times. The first was the morning after we got off the boat. I stood with the other four men he had bought, and he came and looked at us. He was not young and not old. He was the first person I had seen who had eyes the color of the sea. He spoke harshly to Morro, about Abela, I think, and also about the damage to my mouth. Morro kept quiet, staring at the ground, but I could smell his rage. Always after that, when Morro saw me, he would watch me with his hot eyes, looking for some reason to whip me. I never gave him a reason, and that fed his hatred.

One day at the beginning of my fourth year, the colonel came to the mill. He came with a tall black woman, a very proud-looking one wearing a blue turban and a white dress that she hitched up off the ground to keep clean. I didn't know it then, but it was Ma Rosa, who was in charge of the colonel's house. I watched from the corner of my eye while they talked with the boss. Then the boss brought them over to where I was. Ma Rosa stood in front of me, looking me up and down. She asked me some questions, but she was also asking other questions with her eyes. She looked into me. After some silence, she nodded and spoke to the colonel. Then they went away.

The boss said to me, "You safe now, or in shit. I don't know which."

Next day, I started work up at the house.

Time passed, years unfolded, full of things and the names of things. *Saw, wedge, hatchet. Spade, rake, hoe. Charcoal, bellows, anvil, saddle, stirrup; whip* I already knew. *Griddle, kettle, saucepan, jug, flour, pepper. Carpet, chandelier. Goblet, spoon, plate, napkin, tureen.*

One day, there was a big fuss. Ma Rosa roamed among us like a fierce animal. In the afternoon, three boats arrived, and more white people than I had seen since San Juan were carried up the hill. Women as well as men. Meat was roasted in a pit behind the house. I hoped the smell of it wouldn't be unkind enough to drift over to the cabins where we lived.

When the sun was falling, I had to take the slops down to the pigs. When I returned, there was a girl leaning against the wall of the back kitchen looking at the sky and fanning her face with a big leaf. I'd never seen her before, even though she was dressed in house clothes. She had eyes that could smile, and they smiled at me.

Later, when the colonel's guests had eaten and we'd had the leftovers, which were good, there was a revel. There were candles in glass bowls all along the veranda, where the whites sat, flapping their hands at the yellow moths that filled the air. A slave band played, the drummers and a kora

105

player and an old man who played a fiddle holding it against his hip. Behind them all the slaves sat in a big half-circle, and there were tall torches stuck in the ground. Around the edge of the light, Morro and the white gang bosses stood with their guns in their arms and whips in their belts, watching, scratching their crotches.

I was one who brought drinks and fruit and manioc cakes to the white people, and the girl was another. One time I went to the kitchen with a tray and she was there, ladling punch into cups. She stopped when she saw me and stood straight and still. Half her face was gold in the candlelight.

Yes, I remember this.

I asked her name.

She said, "White name Dolores."

I said, "True name?"

She said, "Asuntula."

It was not a name among my people. I had trouble saying it, and she made a little laugh, hiding her mouth behind her hand.

Then she said, "It mean *blessing*."

A magic thing happened next. She reached out and ran her finger softly along my lip, pausing where the kink in it was. The first time, in that life, anyone touched me gently. Inside I felt like trees move in the wind.

She said, "I know your name. Ma Rosa tell me."

"Why she tell you?"

"Because I ask her," she said.

Then she took up the tray of cups and carried them to the door.

I said, "I'll call you Blessing."

She stopped and half turned and dipped her head just a little; then she was gone.

When the band rested, two kegs of watered-down rum were brought around to the front of the house. All the slaves lined up and had one drink, all using the same two cups, drinking and passing the cup on to the next. Then the colonel stood up and said to his guests, "Now the Negroes will entertain us with their African dances."

And they were Worship dances. The women and girls dipped and swayed themselves in a big circle, then in smaller circles, while the men stood tall, stepping then bending. But there was confusion because we were not all one people, and sometimes the drumming stumbled, and the calls were different languages. Most of all, there was no power in the dancing because our ancestors were far, far away. And because the whites were watching, and because Morro and his men were a circle of death around us.

I saw how big my task would be.

A year and a half later, me and Blessing were married at the end of the dry season, when the cane-cutting was almost finished. It was the afternoon of the half-day rest, and the air was heavy under the hot white sky. We were one of four couples married that day. A white priest came upriver and did us as a job lot. We stood in the colonel's partly built church, where the roof timbers cast prison-house shadows. The priest was a short fat man who wore a little black hat and a black robe with a white one over it. His face was melting. His slave stood next to him, holding up a wooden cross with their dead god nailed to it. We were married in a language none of us understood. It did not take long.

When the whites had gone into the house, we held our true ceremonies in the shadowy grove behind the cabins. Ma Rosa had woven eight strong cords of cotton. Each couple held cords in their right hands, and because we had no *pai*, Ma Rosa tied the knots herself. Then Blessing's mother and another mother held a long stick and we stepped over it, two by two. This was not a custom among my people, and I felt foolish doing it; Blessing laughed at the look on my face. We ate corn roasted on the fire and a dish of meat that was the colonel's gift. We drank a fruit-and-rum drink the mill boss had brewed for us. The musicians played, and we danced our different wedding dances as best we could. The children ran wild, and I saw Blessing's eyes following them.

The sun slid behind the trees, a thin disk white as bone. With the darkness came a light rain, hardly more than a mist, that drifted across the grove like thin curtains.

There was a small cabin that was now ours. When we were inside, I saw that Blessing's family had prepared it for us. Two wicks burned in dishes of oil, and the yellow light showed me that our rough bed was covered with a sheet of many colors and patterns that the house girls had sewn. A small bunch of flowers with petals like creamy flesh speckled with blood lay on the sheet. And on the floor around the bed was a line of white pebbles. I looked down at them and then looked at Blessing with a question in my eyes. She smiled and stood with her back to the bed. Her white dress was damp from the rain, and where it stuck to her I could see the beautiful shapeliness of her body. Then sideways with her foot she made a gap in the line of pebbles and said, "Wall is broke, my husband. Come through."

So I reached out and touched her.

Then the door smashed open and evil came in.

The instant I was seized, I smelled Morro's stink. One of the lamps died. Blessing tried to get through the door, but Morro pushed her back. Two men had me by the arms and throat, and a filthy hand covered my mouth. My legs were kicked from under me, and then I was outside in the rain and the darkness that had been a world away. I fought and tried to bite, then something like lightning struck my head. A dark hole opened in front of me and slowly I fell into it, and as I fell I heard Blessing scream.

Then the scream and everything else was far above me and then gone.

When I came back to life, I tried to get onto my knees, but one of the overseers pushed me down again with his foot. I curled up in the wet dust close to the dying fire, and sickness filled my body and my mind.

Some time passed and then I heard Morro call. The overseers went away, leaving their laughter and their pipe smoke hanging in the air.

The cabin door was leaning broken. I held on to the doorpost to keep from falling. Inside, Blessing was huddled in a corner, covering her nakedness with the white dress. Her face was turned away from me, her eyes shut tight, and when I spoke her name, she did not move. The flowers were crushed in the twists of the wedding sheet.

The big rains did not fall for three more weeks. The sky pressed down on us, making the air thick, but did not break. One morning, I went out through the kitchen and saw Morro sitting on a chair in the yard. A house girl named Madelena was cutting his hair. He had his back to me and did not see me. I stood under the lean-to roof for a minute, watching. Then I went inside to the mending room next to Ma Rosa's parlor and took a piece of red thread and a piece of black. I went back out and watched from the shadows till Madelena had finished and showed Morro himself in a mirror. When he went away, Madelena started to sweep up, and I went to her and stopped her. I picked up a lock of Morro's hair and twisted it into a thin greasy cord, doubled it over, and tied it with the red and the black thread. I put it in my pocket.

Madelena watched me with big eyes, but I didn't speak. She didn't speak either, but I knew her, knew she was a mouth and that by the end of the day news of what I had done would be spread among our people in the house and beyond.

Next day, Colonel d'Oliviera and his family set off down the river to San Juan. The colonel's wife was big with their second child, and he wanted her to be near doctors. Truth was, Ma Rosa and her main help, old Ma Perla, knew more about birthing babies than any fool white doctor. Which the colonel got taught cruelly three years later when his wife died giving birth to a girl child. The child died too.

Still, they went, and a fear and quietness spread through the house and the cabins and the village down on the river. Because now Morro was in charge, and whenever the colonel wasn't there to mind him, his drunkenness and fierceness grew.

When the dark began to fill the forest, I took a gourd cup to the butchering shed and filled it with pig blood that was thickening for sausage. I took it to the kitchen and set it down on the big cooking table. Blessing was there, cleaning up with two other women and two boys, the ones who carried out the slops. They all watched me as I went to the kitchen store and filled a dish with salt and took one of the thin black cheroots that Ma Rosa liked to smoke. I stood the cup of blood on the dish of salt and put the cheroot in my pocket. Then I went to the cooking grills and collected hot charcoals on a little iron shovel. I took all these things outside and walked slow and steady through the cabins, knowing I was watched but not looking at those who watched me. It was near dark now.

At the edge of the grove, where the long arms of the trees stretched out, I collected dry stuff and heaped it on the coals and blew till flame licked up. I swept a little patch of earth clean with the edge of my hand. I dribbled the blood in a square shape, and inside that square I made another of salt. I took out the fetish I had made of Morro's hair and put it, careful and exact, in the center. Then with an unburnt coal, I drew a long mark down my left cheek, and with the last of the blood from the bowl, I drew a long mark down my right cheek. I sat and lit the cheroot from the fire and blew smoke in all the ten directions and began my chant, softly, rocking my body.

Did Maco come to me? I still cannot say. I had no strong trust in myself, felt I had little strength, little wisdom. I was very young, and so far away. Maybe the *pai* had poured his teaching into a leaky cup. I was steering my soul on strange waters with no stars to guide me. What I can say is this: that first time, Maco did not grow in me the way he did later. He did not spread inside me like a skin spreading under my own skin, making me a shape he could live in. No. If I saw him, his face half red and half black, watching through his closed eyes, it was like seeing him as a shadow on glass. And I was where I was: I sensed people gathering in the darkness beyond the small light of the fire, as I knew they would. But I chanted on, and I smoked on, the taste of the tobacco making sickness rise in my throat. And when I thought it was right, I threw Morro's hair onto the fire.

It burned stench, like the smell from sores, like something left dead to rot in the swamp. Groans and soft cries then came from the darkness around me. I made one last veneration, strong as I could, then I stood and rubbed away the blood and salt with my foot. I walked to my cabin, not looking at the people parting to let me pass.

After a while Blessing came in and stood with her back against the door.

"Husband," she said, "what you done? Who you think you are?"

Next day and the next, I saw that people looked at Morro in a different way. Not scared of him, but scared for him. It gave me a quiet joy.

On the third day, the sun did not rise. Instead, the rain finally came, at first slow fat splashes, then so fast and thick you thought you could not walk through it.

About noontime, Ma Rosa came out back and said, "Morro is here. On the veranda in his damn dirty boots like he own the place."

She looked at me stern. "And you stay away from him," she said in a voice that was both hard and soft.

But when she wasn't looking, I slipped into the big room at the front of the house and watched him through the glass doors. He was sprawled sideways in the colonel's hammock, pulling the flesh from fried chicken and drinking rum and coconut milk, staring into the rain.

The rain stopped halfway through the afternoon, and the clouds slid away like a sheet pulled from a bed. I went and stood on the back steps down into the yard to breathe the fresh-washed air. Light in splinters came off the trees and the air was riot with birdsong and frog call. One of the young yard boys came splashing through the red mud, leading Morro's horse around to the front of the house. I went to the glass doors and watched Morro ride off, watched him turn the horse down the hill toward the river.

I knew where he was going. Alongside the jetty was a big stone house with bars on all the windows. One half was boat repair, one half the store. Morro and the white overseers liked to spend nights in there with the store boss, drinking and gambling. Usually they kept themselves pretty quiet. But when the colonel was away, they sometimes got worked up loud and wild, and dragged our women in there, and fired their guns out of the windows to make a scare.

That night I waited till I knew Blessing was asleep, and then I stole out. The moon was fat and everywhere was black and silver-blue. I moved from shadow to shadow through the cabins, then on down the hill. I cut left through the trees and came out on the track that went from the buildings on the river along to the barrack house where Morro and the other overseers lived. Near where I came out, the track crossed a little creek on a bridge made of thick planks. In the dry season, there was just a trickle in the creek, but now it was already full, the water up to the underbelly of the planks and spread out over the track and into the bushes.

I got the knotted wedding cord out of my pocket. I took off my light-color clothes and hid them in a mostly dry place under some big wide leaves. Then I melted naked into the darkness under the trees.

It was a long wait but I was not restless. My blood ran cool and peaceful, and my heart went steady like the slow tick of the colonel's big stand-up clock.

I heard the horse first, going *brrr-brrr* with its lips, then Morro mumbling a song mixed with curses. I looked down to the bridge, and the horse came into the moonlight there with Morro swaying on its back. When it got to the flood, it stopped and would not go on, even though Morro kicked it in the belly with his heels. In the end he slid off the horse and stood crooked, cursing some more. I could see now that he had a brown clay bottle in one hand. He splashed and staggered onto the bridge, hauling on the reins, and after much trouble, he got the horse to walk onto it and across.

Now he was close to me. I could see he was bewildered because he knew he was too drunk to get back into the saddle. I took one silent step toward him. He pulled the stopper from the bottle and lifted it to his mouth. While he was still swallowing, I stepped up behind him and looped the wedding cord over his head down onto his throat. I crossed my hands and pulled tight. Such strength I had then! He made a sound like sucking mud, and rum came out of his nose.

I pulled his head back and whispered in his ear, "This is for Blessing."

When his hands and legs went useless, I dragged him back to the creek and drowned him.

Like I expected, the news came up to the house early the next day. Ma Rosa was still telling us our work when she was called out. Morro had fallen drunk from his horse and drowned in the creek, she told us. Her face tried to keep cloud in it, but the sun kept breaking through. She didn't look at me.

Later, when the rain was coming down heavy again, I had to go into the kitchen and Madelena was there. She went on one knee and took my hand and placed it on top of her head.

"*Pai,*" she said. Just that one word.

We were like that when I looked over to the entry into the hall and Blessing was standing outside it. She watched for two heartbeats, then closed the door.

So that was how I began. With a vengeance.

FOUR: DEAD MAN'S LANDING

The Cathedral Church of Saint Francis contained more gold and silver than any other church in Latin America, according to the leaflet Faustino had picked up at the entrance. The saint's side chapel alone boasted more than sixty pounds of gold leaf, which, laid flat, would cover three soccer fields. Standing at the elaborate railing that separated the chapel from grubby worshippers, Faustino figured that would be about right. The far wall was a vast and grotesque fantasy coated in the stuff. A horde of pouting golden cherubs with plump golden buttocks hovered around golden niches within which golden madonnas suckled golden baby Christs. From below, gold pillars erupted into golden birds, flowers, weirdly imagined animals. (What were those? Faustino wondered. Camels? Turtles on stilts?) Golden plants writhed around forms and faces that choked on gold. And there in the middle of it all was Saint Francis himself, who'd taught that poverty and simplicity were the surest routes to God. He was wearing a plain brown habit and was looking upward, startled, as if to say, "Jesus, what the hell happened?" If he'd asked Faustino that question, Faustino would have said, "Well, Frank, it looks for all the world like some really big guy ate a mix of plaster and gold dust and threw up all over your wall." But Faustino was hungover and in a sour mood.

Faustino glanced at his watch: ten past ten. A creased and ancient woman appeared at his side. She closed her eyes and began a murmured prayer to the saint, although, from the look of her, she didn't need any tips from Francis on how to live a life of poverty. Faustino ambled back to the central aisle, looking out at the main doors, which today were fully opened. Worshippers were beginning to assemble for Mass; a jumble of fractured and mingling silhouettes moved among the glare. Two of them became distinct as they approached: Edson Bakula and a young girl.

She was, Faustino guessed, fourteen or thereabouts. Breasts budding beneath the pink T-shirt. Three-quarter-length cutoff jeans, dusty flip-flops on her feet. Lighter-skinned than Bakula. Her face was strong and handsome rather than pretty, the face of an older person. Faustino extended his hand to Bakula, who, instead of taking it, grasped Faustino's elbow, turning him gently.

"Over here," he said, and led the way along an avenue of

pillars and into a small side chapel. It was deserted apart from a group of soiled marble conquistadors kneeling in embarrassment below a crucified Christ. The girl stood looking up at Faustino, not smiling. Examining his face as if he were a famous person who had turned out to be rather disappointing in real life. Above their heads, thick blades of light from the lancet windows sliced the dim air. Dust motes danced like a million golden flies.

Bakula said quietly, "This is Prima. Primavera de Barros."

Faustino's face began a conventional smile, then froze. *De Barros?*

"She is Brujito's sister. She knows where he is."

Later, much later, Faustino tried to recall what he'd felt at that moment. It wasn't that gleeful uplift, the electrical surge, that a lucky journalist experiences maybe half a dozen times in a working life. That goal-scoring moment of triumph. No, what he remembered was a sort of sudden vertigo. Like walking along an ordinary city pavement and seeing that just ahead it turns into a narrow footpath along the brink of a sheer and infinite precipice. And wanting to turn back but not being able to because the way back, and the city itself, have gone. In fact, at the time, he was immediately and deeply suspicious. But he completed the smile.

"Señorita," he said.

She hesitated, then took his outstretched hand, looking

at their hands joined together as if it were the strangest thing.

Faustino turned to Bakula. "Look, if this —"

But the girl interrupted him. "Rico came home. He was frightened, yeah? He slept one night in the house, then next morning he told Auntie he had to go somewhere an' I followed him. He went to the graveyard. That's how I know where he is. There's only one place you can go from there."

She spoke rhythmically, like someone speaking the words of a song while trying to ignore the tune. Or like someone reciting something that has been rehearsed. Her voice was husky, low-pitched, with a strong, almost Caribbean, accent.

"Rico?"

"Ricardo," Bakula said. "Brujito."

"Right."

The girl said, "I came to find Edson. He said to talk to you."

She stood looking at Faustino like somebody lost and helpless but also stubborn, as if she were a foreigner insisting on being understood. It annoyed him.

"OK, when was this? When did your brother go home?"

"Night after that game. The one when he got took off."

Faustino looked at her, waiting for some small sign of embarrassment, perhaps, or guilt, but there was none. He turned to Bakula.

"This is some kind of joke, right?"

"No."

"No? What then? A scam? There's shit breaking loose all over the country about this thing, and suddenly you pop up with the kid's sister? Come on, Edson."

"We're telling you the truth, Paul."

The girl's gaze switched back and forth between the men's faces.

A thought, an ugly one, occurred to Faustino. He said to her harshly, "Did you try this on Max Salez?"

"Señor?"

"Maximo Salez. Another journalist. Like me. Did you tell him this story?"

"I don' know no one called that. I ain't told no one 'cept Edson."

Bakula said, "Prima didn't get to San Juan until yesterday evening. She came on the late boat."

Boat? Faustino's head swarmed with questions that the sensible part of his brain didn't want answered. He wondered fleetingly if in San Juan it was all right to smoke in church.

"OK, Prima," he said, "tell me this. Everyone's been looking for Brujito for nearly two weeks. So why haven't you gone to the police?"

She looked at him as if he had spoken in a strange language. Then, glancing briefly at Bakula, she said, "No police."

Faustino sighed through his nose and raised his eyes

heavenward. He found himself looking at Jesus. The sculptor had been at pains to depict the agony of crucifixion. The tortured body seemed on the verge of coming apart under its own weight. The fingers were hooked into claws as if trying to pluck at the spikes through their palms, and the wound in the side had ragged, pouting lips. The face, though, wore a bland, almost blank, expression. Or was that the ghost of a slightly skeptical smile?

Faustino was startled when the girl expressed what he was feeling.

"I don' like it here, Edson," she said.

"No? We can go somewhere else. Is that all right with you, Paul?"

"Sure. You go wherever you want. I've got things to do."

Faustino then made the mistake of looking at Prima's face.

"Please, Señor," she said.

Her eyes were wide and moist. Faustino could detect no trace of guile in them. He looked at his watch, then shrugged and said, "OK."

Which turned out to be a second mistake.

Bakula led them into the labyrinth of streets and alleys behind the cathedral. The ways were narrow and crowded, filled with a soft cacophony of competing music and the heavy odor of food frying in palm oil. At a door unmarked by any sign, Bakula halted and politely stood aside to allow Faustino to enter first.

Just inside, a very large and very black woman sat behind a counter, watching a soap opera on a tiny portable TV set. She wore a white turban and a green T-shirt printed with a portrait of Nelson Mandela. Stretched across the vast balcony of her chest, Mandela's face was distorted into something grinning and oriental, a cartoon Buddha. When she saw Bakula, she raised her hand. Faustino figured that her upper arm was pretty much the same girth as his thigh, but the flesh on it didn't tremble when she slapped her palm against Bakula's in a lazy high five.

At the back of the shop, a doorway, curtained with a rainbow of plastic ribbons, opened onto a small walled courtyard. A greeny-blue plastic tarpaulin had been rigged up as an awning; it cast a cool submarine light down onto the half-dozen white tables and the dozen white chairs. Bakula brought a third chair to the table in the far corner, and they all sat down.

Faustino was damned if he was going to initiate any conversation, so he lit a cigarette, crossed his legs, and surveyed his surroundings. The only other customers were two men sitting at the table closest to the door. One was tall and lean; the other — the older one with the bandanna on his head — was shorter and stockier. Both had muscles where normal people don't. They paid no attention to Faustino and his companions; the younger guy was fiddling with a cell phone while the other watched attentively, as if receiving a silent lesson in modern technology.

The voice of Bob Marley began to warble softly from a pair of wall-mounted speakers. Prima murmured along with the song, her eyes down, watching her feet.

The big Mandela-chested woman emerged from the shop carrying a tray. She unloaded it onto the table: a glass jug of what looked like mango juice, a Pepsi, three tumblers, a plate of fried bean rissoles, and a dish of innocent-looking green salsa, which, Faustino knew, would light the fires of hell in his mouth if he were fool enough to taste it. Prima had no such qualms; she began to eat enthusiastically.

When the woman had returned to her soap opera, Bakula said, "Paul, I realize this will seem . . . strange."

Faustino raised his eyebrows and harrumphed smoke from his nose.

"But I assure you that Prima is telling the truth. She believes her brother's life is in danger. She came to San Juan to see if I could help."

"Why you?"

Prima swallowed and said, "Auntie told me Edson's one person in San Juan we can trust."

"Really?"

Bakula said, "Prima's aunt is someone I know quite well. Santo Tomas is a place I visit from time to time."

"And where is that?"

"Half a day by boat, up the Rio Verde."

"Ah," Faustino said. "In the Cane Country."

"Yes."

Faustino turned back to the girl, caught her before she could put more food in her face. "And you say that's where your brother is? In Santo Tomas?"

"Not exac'ly. Close by."

"OK. So why doesn't he just come back to San Juan? Why's he hiding out in the bush somewhere?"

She didn't look at him. "He's not hidin'," she said eventually. "He can't leave."

"What do you mean, he can't leave? Are you saying he's been kidnapped?"

She seemed unable to answer. She looked away and murmured something Faustino couldn't catch.

"Yes," Bakula said. "He's been kidnapped."

"Well, now," Faustino said pleasantly. "We seem to have a problem here. I happen to know that Ricardo walked away from the DSJ stadium unaccompanied. And in the cathedral, Prima, you told me that he came home and slept in the house, then in the morning went off somewhere—a graveyard, I think you said? And I assume he was alone, is that right?"

"Yeah," Prima said sulkily. She glanced at Bakula. "But he said he was expected, tho."

"I'm not an expert, of course," Faustino admitted, "but that doesn't sound like any kind of kidnapping I've heard of. Actually, it sounds for all the world like someone doing something of his own free will."

In the absence of an ashtray, he tapped ash onto the floor.

"You know, Edson, after a few years in my trade, you develop a nose for bullshit. I can smell it now. I can smell it quite strongly, as a matter of fact. Why don't you tell me what you want?"

Bakula did not seem offended. He nodded thoughtfully. "You're right, of course. We're not telling you all of it. It does sound as though Ricardo was acting out of what you call free will. But he wasn't. Prima thinks—I think—that he was terrified."

"Terrified? Of what?"

Prima looked at him then, and Faustino was dismayed to see that her eyes were wet.

"He think his spirit's hex. But it ain't so. I know it ain't so." She shook her head grievously. A teardrop landed on Faustino's wrist. He resisted the desire to wipe it away but leaned away from her, discomforted.

"Is a shittin' trick, man. Tell him, Edson. Tell him."

Her voice was suddenly hard and fierce despite the tears. The two men at the far table glanced in her direction, then away again.

Bakula reached across the table and snapped the can of Pepsi open. Crack and hiss. He wrapped Prima's hand around it, saying, "Shh. Be cool. Drink this. It's all right."

Behind and above the girl's head, a small green-and-yellow lizard scuttled to a new position on the wall and froze.

Prima sniffed, staring at the keyhole into her Pepsi.

Bakula said, "We need your help, Paul. The problem is, we are dealing here with things you don't believe in."

Faustino looked blank for a moment or two, then nodded wisely, as if at a gradual revelation.

"Oh, I *see*. So we aren't talking about just any old kidnapping here. We're talking about voodoo kidnapping. Is that right? Prima reckons her brother is bewitched?"

The girl made a sound, *"Huh,"* which was somehow contemptuous and despairing at the same time.

Bakula looked away briefly, then said, "*Bewitched* is not a word that we, I, would use, but . . ." He seemed affected by tiredness suddenly and made a visible effort to overcome it.

"Ricardo's aunt's house is a Veneration house. You understand? A place of Worship. The children were brought up rather strictly. Ricardo is particularly devout. He believes, for example, that his skill as a player is a spiritual gift. Literally. And that anything harmful to his spirit will damage his ability. That's been a source of strength for him. Until now. Prima thinks someone, some people, have convinced—"

Here Prima again muttered something that Faustino couldn't make out, and Bakula laid his hand on her wrist to quiet her.

"Prima is sure that Ricardo believes his spirit has been separated from him. That he is being controlled. She is sure that nothing else can explain what happened."

The plastic ribbons across the doorway rustled, and another big man, wearing violet-tinted sunglasses, came into the yard. He joined the other two. Elaborate manual greetings were performed, and the man in the bandanna chuckled. It was a rich, attractive sound, a subterranean river running over dark stones. It seemed to Faustino that their company would be more fun than what he was stuck with. *In four hours, I'll be on a plane out of here,* he thought.

He said, "May I ask you a question?"

"Please do."

"Why are you telling me this?"

"We want you to write the story. To publish the truth in your paper."

For a second or two, it was as though Faustino had not heard. He sat back in his chair, smiling as if at some mildly amusing anecdote. Bakula watched him, expressionless. Prima sat hunched over her Pepsi, blinking at it; she looked like a hapless child trapped in a tedious adult conversation that had nothing to do with her.

"It's a big story, Paul."

Faustino stopped smiling. "Really? I had no idea."

"I'm sorry. Of course, I mean—"

Faustino raised a hand, a halt gesture, then put it flat on the table and leaned forward.

"Go to the police, Edson," he said quietly and solemnly. "Really. If you believe what Prima has told you, go to the police. I don't know how powerful this voodoo stuff is, but I wouldn't mind betting that a SWAT team with a load of automatic weapons and a bunch of tear gas would sort it out."

Bakula sipped from his glass, then put it back down precisely on the wet ring it had left on the table. He gazed into Faustino's eyes; in the filtered light under the awning, the shaded half of his face was greenish.

Very calmly he said, "Paul, Ricardo has been missing for fourteen days. In all that time, no police officers have been seen in Santo Tomas, despite the fact they must know it's where he comes from and that Prima and his aunt live there. Why might that be, do you think?"

133

"I haven't the faintest idea," Faustino said, then found that he did. The answer popped bright as sunrise—a sunrise that Bakula had conjured—into Faustino's head. The police hadn't gone up the river to look for Brujito *because they already knew he was there. Because they were responsible for him being there.*

Bakula was still watching Faustino's eyes; now he nodded slightly.

"Yes," he said. "There is more to this than what you call mumbo jumbo. It's a bigger story than you thought."

"I see."

"And what that means, we think, is that Ricardo will not be set free. Even if the da Silvas agree to a ransom demand, no matter how big it is. Because of what he knows. Because he might talk. He *would* talk, I imagine. He's not the most . . . sophisticated boy in the world."

"He's a fool to his own damn self," Prima said softly.

"There are perhaps other ways of releasing Ricardo," Bakula said. "But even then, he would not be safe, especially if he returned to San Juan. Unless . . ."

"Unless what?"

Bakula nipped his lower lip thoughtfully, then said, "We are a long way from anywhere up here, Paul. Can you remember when you last saw national TV coverage of anything that happened in San Juan? Apart from soccer or carnival? When did *La Nación* last run a story about anything up here, before this?"

134

"The point being?"

"The point being that if a recently released kidnapped soccer star from San Juan suddenly turned up dead in an alley behind a crack house or floating facedown in the river, it would get maybe a page on the first day, a paragraph on the second day, then nothing. Right?"

"Maybe."

"No maybe about it. A national uproar, a great demand for justice? I don't think so. And in this city, there's not exactly a long tradition of policemen arresting other policemen. Most of the Anti-Corruption Squad have been suspended for two years, charged with corruption."

"I don't think I like the way this is heading," Faustino said.

"The reality is, Paul, that Ricardo's life isn't worth shit unless the people who've got him get put away for a very long time. Along with the people protecting them. Believe me, that won't happen unless the world is watching to see that it happens. We need the glare of publicity."

Faustino grimaced at the cliché, but Bakula was undeterred. "*National* publicity. And for it to stay there, shining on the wicked until they are gone."

"Oh, come on, Bakula."

"I'm perfectly serious. That's why we need your help. You have the power to summon them up, the media, the really big shots. The nationals. We do not. Who's going to listen to *us*?"

Faustino felt a tingle in his lower body: excitement, perhaps, or perhaps just cramp. For a second or two his professional lust for a great story warred with his instinct for survival, but then he recalled Captain Varga's icy smile, the photograph of Max's waterlogged corpse. He shifted on the hard seat.

"Your faith in my influence is flattering," he said. "And misguided. Let me tell you a few things, just to put you in touch with reality." He held his hand up again, this time to count off points on his fingers. "First: I'm not your man. I am not a crime reporter. In fact, right now, I'm not a reporter at all. I'm working on a book, and that's keeping me fully occupied. Second: Maximo Salez was covering this story, and he ended up with a knife in his chest. Whether the two things are connected or not, I have no intention of occupying the mortuary slab next to his. Third: Last night I booked myself on this afternoon's flight home, and I have *every* intention of being on it. Fourth, and last but not least: The fact is that I have no reason to believe a word you've told me. Call me a cynic, but saying something's the truth don't make it so."

"I understand that," Bakula said. "Which is why we want you to come to Santo Tomas with us."

"You're out of your mind," Faustino stated. Calmly, as if it were a scientific fact. "And if you want my considered opinion, you're getting into something way over your head. Stick to being a tour guide. You're pretty good at that."

He stood, and Prima looked up at him. The expression on her face was odd, Faustino thought, almost as though she felt sorry for him, rather than herself.

"Paul," Bakula said. "Please reconsider. There are flights every day."

"Yep, and I'm getting today's. Good luck, and thanks for the hospitality."

The three men at the far table got up and went to stand by the door. The curtains parted and they were joined by a fourth, equally powerful man, then by the huge proprietress. They all looked at Faustino, their faces full of solemn sympathy like people watching a disabled person attempt something overambitious.

"Bakula? What the hell is this?"

Bakula sighed. "I'm sorry, Paul."

The woman smiled. A big arc of white teeth, apart from the canines, which were gold.

She said to Faustino, "Me sons. Mateo, Marcos, Lucas, Juan. You'll be OK with them. They'll watch over you. Nothing to worry 'bout."

Gently, Marcos drove his minibus into a part of San Juan that Faustino hadn't known existed and wouldn't have gone to if he had: a swarming network of creeks and piers, of puddled streets and soot-smeared sheds. At one point, where Marcos took a sudden left, the vast and rusting hull of a ship reared up just beyond a row of ramshackle buildings. Men hung against it in terrifying cradles, welding. Sparks, small electrical blizzards, flurried among them.

Marcos parked in an area of oil-stained concrete where other vehicles — mostly pickup trucks and small motorbikes rigged with trailers — stood abandoned. His passengers climbed out and followed Prima through a short sequence of narrow alleyways. If the gringo hadn't looked so sullen, they might have been taken for an oddly assorted group setting out for a picnic on one of the islands. Mateo, the eldest brother, the one with the bandanna, had an orange cooler perched on his head; he supported it casually with two fingers. Lucas had a big backpack slung over one shoulder, Bakula a smaller one; Marcos carried a large Nike sports bag. Faustino walked closely alongside Juan because their wrists were fastened together by a thick plastic strap.

They emerged onto a flagstoned pier overlooking a channel crowded with boats. Many were derelict, tilted onto the muddy shallows as if by some ancient gale, their timbers sprung from their ribs, their innards rusting. The water looked thick and gray, except where it had a prismatic skin of oil. Green coconuts and plastic bottles bobbed in it.

From the pier a wide gangway sloped down onto a floating pontoon to which working boats were tethered. There was a good deal of human traffic and business. The pier was piled here and there with engine parts, crates of fruit and vegetables, butane gas bottles. At one end of the pontoon, a man in a blood-smeared jersey was cleaning fish, taking them from a wooden tray, slitting them open, flicking the guts into the water. He seemed oblivious to the screaming cloud of gulls he'd summoned. Faustino and his abductors descended the gangway; a number of people nodded greetings to Prima, glancing at Faustino and away again.

On the pontoon, Marcos made his farewells. He held Prima's head in his huge hands and kissed her forehead, shook hands respectfully with Bakula, clasped hands with each of his brothers. Finally he touched Faustino lightly on the shoulder.

"You'll be OK with these guys, man."

"I was even more OK without them," Faustino said sourly.

Marcos looked slightly hurt. He turned and gave Faustino a reproachful glance before climbing the gangway.

The boat was called *El Peregrino*, and it looked almost seaworthy. It was about twenty feet long, with a three-sided wheelhouse toward the bow and an awning over the middle section of the deck. Lucas squeezed himself into the wheelhouse. Mateo went to a wooden deck locker and undid the two heavy padlocks that held it shut. He put the bags and the cooler into it, then took out a number of thin foam cushions, which he spread in the shade. That done, he busied himself with the ropes that lashed *El Peregrino* to the pontoon. Bakula and Prima sat cross-legged on the cushions. Juan sat himself down on the bench that ran the length of the boat, on the side farthest from the dock. Because he couldn't do otherwise, Faustino sat next to him.

"Mind if I smoke?"

"Is bad for you," Juan said.

"I'll take that as a *yes,* then," Faustino said, fumbling left-handed in his jacket pocket.

The boat's engine coughed and rumbled, then steadied into an eager roar. Faustino felt it through his feet. Mateo called to Lucas, moving quickly toward the stern. The bow swung outward, the engine settled into a heavy beat—

coarser than Faustino would have liked — and the pontoon receded. At the moment that Lucas brought the boat into midstream, all the churches of San Juan set up a clamor of Sunday bells.

The waterway twisted like a gut. In some places it was no wider than a city street, with ancient and improvised buildings looming over it. Like Venice, perhaps, Faustino thought. If Venice had been torched and looted. In other places it was broad, fringed with stilted jetties.

After twenty minutes or so, the jumbled silhouette of a broken fortress appeared on the north bank, and then, suddenly and miraculously, they were in the bay. The sky became vast and the air surged; Faustino felt his face freckled by saltwater droplets. *El Peregrino* began to buck and shudder in the onshore swell. Off to the left, the city of San Juan occupied the entire horizon: a barricade of white and ocher towers between the green-blue sea and the gray-blue sky.

Lulled by the tip and slide of the boat and by the pulse of its engine, Faustino found himself losing consciousness. After twitching awake a few times, he surrendered and went under. At one point he heard or dreamed Bakula's voice close to his ear, saying, "These same waves have lapped the shores of Africa." When he awoke — embarrassed to realize he'd slept with his head on Juan's massive shoulder — the world had changed.

They were on the Rio Verde. The river was indeed green, a soft green, the color of an olive. It looked almost half a mile wide. On the north bank, there was nothing but vegetation, like a continuous low green cloud along the horizon of water; beyond it, vague in the hard sunlight, crests of taller forest trees arose then fell away. Turning his head, Faustino saw that on the south bank there were still signs of primitive civilization: small clusters of tin-roofed shacks squeezed into gaps in the trees, boats pulled up onto narrow silt beaches, the occasional thin column of smoke. Of the great and sprawling city of San Juan, there was no sign whatsoever.

Prima was kneeling on the cushions, peeling and slicing fruit onto a flattened plastic bag. Bakula lay close to her, on his side, his head cupped in his hand. Their murmured conversation was lost behind the sound of the boat's engine.

Mateo was reclining on the locker, smiling across at Faustino.

"OK, Señor?"

Faustino was not OK. His backside and left leg were numb. Someone had lined his mouth with Velcro.

"I'm thirsty," he said.

Mateo looked at Juan, who shrugged, then he swung his legs onto the deck. He took a clasp knife from his pocket and flipped it open; the blade looked hefty enough to butcher a cow. Mateo held the tip of it close to Faustino's nose.

"Are you a good swimmer, Señor Paul?"

"What? No."

Mateo's smile broadened. He stooped and sliced through the strap that bound Faustino's wrist to Juan's; then he closed the knife by swiping it against his thigh.

Faustino got to his feet and stood lopsided, clutching an awning rope. Mateo rummaged in the locker and took out a plastic bottle, which he tossed to Faustino. The water was cold, and Faustino drank half of it. He looked at his watch. By now he would've—should've—been at the airport, finishing a last gin and tonic in the first-class section of the departure lounge. He went and sat at the stern, watching *El Peregrino*'s green wake fan out and fade. Self-pity was as tempting as a warm bath. He looked into the shade of the awning and saw Bakula observing him, so he inhaled deeply and straightened himself. *To hell with you, man.*

So. Maybe there *was* a story to be had out of this.

MY KIDNAPPING HELL, *by Paul Faustino.*

Too tabloid.

THE RELUCTANT TOURIST. *In the Deep North to research his forthcoming book on the legendary El Gato, top sportswriter Paul Faustino is lured to an obscure backstreet bar. So begins his nightmare journey into the dark badlands of Kidnapping Country. Read the full story in* La Nación Weekend *this Saturday.*

Something like that.

Or maybe even HOW I FOUND BRUJITO AND LIVED TO TELL THE TALE.

But there was at least one improbability in that title. . . .

He felt the bench shift. Prima was sitting next to him, proffering fruit in a plastic dish: trimmed chunks of pineapple and guava, crescents of melon.

"No, thanks."

"It's good for you. If you smoke, you should eat plentya fruit."

"I find it deeply touching that everyone is so concerned about my health."

She continued to regard him solemnly; it seemed she had no grasp of irony, but then she said, "We don' want you to come to no harm, Señor Paul."

"Hah!"

She set the bowl down on the bench between them. Faustino expected her to leave him, but she sat studying the deck, her hands clasped between her knees.

"Prima," he said, "you do know that this could get you

into a world of trouble, don't you? As far as I know, there are still laws against abduction in this state. You could get put in jail, even at your age."

Without looking up, she said, "We wanted you to come voluntary."

Faustino appeared to consider this seriously. "Somehow, I don't think that's going to sound convincing in a court of law."

She didn't reply. So Faustino sighed and turned his upper body toward her, laying his arm along the back of the bench. His fingertips were close to her shoulder.

Quietly he said, "OK, let's not worry about that. The fact is, I'm here. You've got me. And I don't suppose that what's-his-name is going to turn the boat around no matter how nicely I ask him."

"Lucas," she said.

"Yeah. So why don't you tell me what this is really about?"

Her eyes flickered up. Bakula was now sitting cross-legged, like a yogi, gazing ahead, but there was something in his posture that suggested he was listening, separating murmured words from the throb of the engine.

"Like Edson said. We need a eyewitness. Someone who can get publicity. People die up here, it get hushed up."

"OK, but—"

"Edson says you someone who don' believe somethin' 'less you see it with your eyes."

"That's kind of normal, isn't it? At least, it is where I come from."

She said nothing, just shook her head in a sad sort of way. It annoyed him.

"Is Brujito really your brother?"

It was as if he'd slapped her, made her eyes water. That was better.

Before she could say anything, he said, "OK, OK. I'm sorry. It's just that I don't know what to believe."

She studied his face for a moment. "Yeah. Edson told me that too."

Silently, Faustino heaped obscenities on the man.

He said, "Did you watch Brujito's, your brother's, last game? The one when he —"

"Yeah. On TV."

"So did I. Well, a video of it. It seemed to me that, I don't know, something happened to him. Suddenly. I think he maybe saw something in the crowd. Do you know anything about that?"

She looked down at her feet again. He waited.

"I already told you. Rico believe he got a hex put on him."

"What, in the middle of a game? Why then?"

God, it was like pulling teeth.

After a while she said, "Maybe to show the power of it. Yeah. I think so."

It made some sort of sense, Faustino thought. If sense was joined-up madness. If religion was involved.

146

"All right. But then he went and took the penalty. That, I don't understand."

"He was checkin'. Needed to make sure."

"So if he'd scored, he'd have been OK? Free?"

"Free?" She wasn't agreeing or disagreeing. It was as though she were practicing a word from a foreign language.

They sat silently for a while. Juan lay massively sprawled on the other bench, apparently asleep. Mateo, leaning against the wheelhouse, said something; from within, Lucas laughed. Bakula sat still as a carving, his eyes closed.

Faustino said, "Someone told me that Rico always talked to a *pai* before big games. Do you know who that was?"

"No."

It was obvious this was a lie. Did that mean that up until then she had been telling the truth?

She stood up. "Eat some fruit, Señor Paul," she said. "It's nice."

She went over to Bakula and sat down beside him. He opened his eyes and smiled at her. Faustino selected a wedge of pineapple and bit into it. It was delicious. Spare juice ran down his chin, and he wiped it away hurriedly with the back of his hand before it could drip onto his shirt.

An hour later the river had narrowed and the wilderness had edged closer. One bank was the mirror image of the other: a dense and endless swath of mangroves brooding over their own shadows, stretching their thick spidery legs into the water. The unbroken monotony of the scene and the dead flatness of the water created an illusion of absolute stillness. Despite the steady thump of its engine, *El Peregrino* seemed stationary, locked in place by the slow green current. Only the stubborn movement of the hands of his watch persuaded Faustino that time itself had not come to a standstill.

Prima was now asleep, her knees drawn up close to her chest, her head and shoulders shrouded by Faustino's jacket. Faustino was staring moodily at the treacly drift of water past the boat. He looked up when Bakula settled himself down on the bench beside him.

"I thought you might like a little background on Santo Tomas," Bakula said.

Faustino was damned if he'd admit it. "You thought wrong," he said matter-of-factly.

Bakula was unfazed. "No doubt. But it will help pass the time. Santo Tomas was once the first important place along the Rio Verde. It was founded by Don Tomas d'Oliviera in 1600 or thereabouts. He was a grandee who owned vast amounts of land to the north of the river. He needed a port on the Verde so that he could ship his sugar down to San Juan. And so that his slaves could be shipped up, of course. He chose Santo Tomas because it's where a kink in the river pushes the deep-water channel right up to the north bank. His grandson, another Tomas, built a great mansion there. You can still see traces of it on the hill above the town. The family also tried to build a church, but it was struck by lightning, not once but twice. They took the hint and gave up."

"Fascinating," Faustino said.

"Yes. So, Santo Tomas grew and prospered—well, the town grew and the d'Olivieras prospered—for a couple of hundred years. Then the sugar trade collapsed. The d'Olivieras tried coffee and tobacco instead, but for whatever reason they didn't do well. By this time the family was spending very little time there. They'd built themselves a grand *palacio* in San Juan and left the running of the estates to overseers who probably didn't give a damn as long as they had enough rum to drink and a steady supply of black women to sleep with."

Faustino suspected that he was meant to express his regret for this state of affairs but refused to do so. It wasn't as though he'd enjoyed it personally.

"By about 1900 the d'Olivieras had pretty much given up on the area. It wasn't profitable. Their freed slaves had either drifted away to the city or were trying to scrape a living fishing or sharecropping and couldn't afford to pay their rent most of the time. In 1961 the government bought the estates from Dr. Teodoro d'Oliviera. He got a good price, considering. The fact that Teodoro was a minister in the same government may have had something to do with it. I mention this because when he died, Teodoro left all his worldly goods to his young niece, Flora."

Faustino looked up now, and Bakula smiled.

He said, "I don't think Dr. Teodoro would have approved of his niece's choice of husband. He'd spent most of his political career trying to eliminate people like Gilberto da Silva."

"What the hell are you up to, Edson? What are you using me for?"

Bakula looked regretful. "I'm sorry you see it that way."

"Oh, really? Some other way of looking at it, is there?"

"Yes. I'm not using you. I'm helping you."

Faustino gave an incredulous laugh, which Bakula ignored.

"Or, I should say, we are helping each other. After all, we are both in the business of enlightening people. In our different ways. Besides, I don't think you are being completely honest with me. Or yourself. When we were talking in the café earlier, I felt sure that a part of you wanted to do this. Your instinct. Was I wrong?"

Faustino declined to answer. A hundred yards away, something detached itself from the darkness beneath the mangroves and entered the water, casting thick ripples that then closed over it.

Bakula resumed his lecture as though it had not been interrupted. "For many of us," he said, "what's important about Santo Tomas is not its glorious past, nor its wretched present. What matters is the place's association with Paracleto."

He paused, waiting for a response. When none came, he asked, "Does the name mean anything to you?"

Faustino noted the slight change in Bakula's tone. And his facial expression. There was something almost beseeching in it. Faustino imagined that certain — perhaps most — women would have found it irresistible. He put on a show of reluctant interest.

"It rings a distant bell. Wasn't he the guy that led the big slave revolt in — what was it? — 1850 or something? Or was that some other *eto*?"

"It's rather complicated. It's true that the rebellion began on the d'Oliviera estates. That's what happened to the house; it was burned down. But Paracleto is a name that legends attach themselves to. It's a sort of nickname, you might say." Bakula faked a smile. "I'm surprised that none of your soccer stars have used it. Anyway, some people say that Paracleto was several different people; others believe he never existed. In fact, the first recorded use of the name dates from 1789. It's in a letter from the bishop of San Juan to Colonel Sebastian d'Oliviera. The bishop wanted to know why Sebastian was apparently allowing 'heathen African practices' to take place on his estate. It's a stern letter. It refers to the 'so-called *pai,* or priest, Paracleto,' and to 'lewd ceremonies conducted by him in the depths of the night in which our Lord Jesus Christ is mocked.'

"Don Sebastian's reply has also survived. In the politest language, he gives the bishop the finger. He says that Paracleto is a man 'possessed of a deeply religious spirit who commands the respect of all the other Negroes.' He also says that Paracleto is 'greatly skilled in the arts of healing.' It seems that in the previous year there had been another outbreak of cholera along the river, and Paracleto had saved the lives of a good many of Sebastian's slaves, and those of Sebastian's two sons, Felipe and Luis. The letter talks about his 'courageous, unsleeping, and tender nursing of the sick,' and about his great knowledge of herbal remedies. And so on. At one point he uses the word 'wise' to describe Paracleto, which would have been a pretty provocative thing to say about an African slave back then. Especially to a bishop."

"Really. He have anything to say about these lewd goings-on in the jungle?"

"Yes. He says that as a mark of his gratitude to Paracleto, he allowed him to build what the letter calls 'a hermitage' outside Santo Tomas. A place where Paracleto would sometimes retreat to for the purpose of 'prayer and contemplation.' That's what d'Oliviera called it, I suppose because it might sound better to the bishop. It's more likely that Paracleto went there to do what in Veneration is called 'remembering.'"

"That would be getting in touch with the ancestors, at a guess."

"More or less. Sebastian says that on certain feast days — he doesn't say which — his Negroes have his permission to attend religious ceremonies at Paracleto's hermitage. He denies that these are 'heathen rituals.' He says that he had himself attended two of these ceremonies, and on both occasions they were conducted 'in a seemly, sober, and dignified manner.'"

"How very disappointing," Faustino said regretfully.

Bakula ignored him. "D'Oliviera also says that while it is true that at these ceremonies the slaves would speak in their 'barbarous African tongues,' they devoutly worshipped the Blessed Virgin Mary and other saints venerated by the Holy Catholic Church. He ends the letter by saying, in a very elaborate way, that he doesn't give a hoot what the bishop thinks anyway, because since his slaves started

153

going to Paracleto's hermitage, they'd been much easier to manage."

"This doesn't sound like the kind of guy who'd start a revolt," Faustino said.

"If it had been the same Paracleto, he'd have been at least a hundred years old by 1850."

"A bit long in the tooth for massacring and pillaging."

"A bit, perhaps," Bakula agreed. "Although when the army crushed the uprising, they captured a very old man who called himself Paracleto and brought him back to San Juan. They couldn't decide whether to hang him or burn him, so they did both. They lit a bonfire beneath the gallows, put a rope around his neck, and dropped him into it. It attracted a big crowd. The story goes, though, that it wasn't Paracleto but one of his followers who allowed himself to be martyred so that the real Paracleto could escape. It may be so. There were reports of appearances in Santo Tomas and elsewhere soon after the execution. I have seen a photograph of a *pai* named Paracleto taken in 1924, and another taken in 1958. I am quite sure that both were taken at the site of the original hermitage near Santo Tomas."

It was the arithmetic of lunacy, but before Faustino could say anything, Bakula said, "There have been impostors, of course. Liars, opportunists, con men, thieves, politicians, blasphemers. Those who think masks are to hide behind, not see through. But they are like leeches — greedy and ugly but not difficult to remove."

There was no mistaking the suppressed anger in his voice.

Faustino flicked his cigarette butt into the river.

"You know what?" he said. "I'm beginning to think you're as crazy as a bottled wasp."

Prima knelt at the prow of the boat. Lucas held the engine at quarter speed, watching her signals. In the east, the sky was deepening into indigo; to the west, it was a lurid orange smear printed over with the flat black shapes of the highest trees. The thought struck Faustino — and he wished it hadn't — that it looked like one of Max Salez's shirts. The river had taken on a peculiar bronze color. The wall of mangroves was now broken by densely shadowed creeks and sudden upthrusts of rock. It was just beyond one of these that Lucas spun the wheel hard and put the engine into reverse. *El Peregrino* swung, straightened, eased forward again, and slipped into a narrow inlet. It was not much more than twice the length of the boat and ended in dense vegetation crowding onto a small silt beach. The air smelled of decay.

Lucas cut the engine. Mateo, at the stern, lobbed the anchor into the water and hauled on the rope until the boat was motionless. Prima leaped onto the little beach and lashed the prow rope to a gnarled protruding root.

Faustino said, "What now?"

"We wait for night and the moon," Bakula said. "And while we're waiting, we'll eat. We missed lunch, remember?" Something in his tone suggested he held Faustino responsible for this misfortune.

Juan went to the locker and lifted out the cooler. He brought it over to where Faustino was sitting and sat down.

"Good food," he said. "Mama make it herself. You got any complaints, you speak to her 'bout it."

"I'm sure it will be first class. Any chance of a gin and tonic before dinner?"

"Is bad for you," Juan said.

The food was, in fact, as good as anything Faustino had tasted since leaving the capital. While they ate, darkness filled the inlet. Looking up, he was entranced, despite himself. He could not remember when he had last seen a sky so softly black or stars so close; they looked near enough to gather by the handful.

The pulsing electronic warble of frogs paused then swelled again when Lucas restarted *El Peregrino*'s engine and eased the boat out into the main stream. Faustino was puzzled to see a track of light running upriver; he knew Lucas had not switched on the boat's lamp. Then he turned and saw the rising moon, a yellow dome above the ragged fringe of trees.

Twenty long minutes later, lights glimmered ahead and to the right. They disappeared, and then were there again, closer.

"Santo Tomas," Prima said, suddenly beside him. She was now wearing some dark garment over her T-shirt.

The lights formed themselves into strings and clusters; Faustino could just make out a clutter of roofs and paler walls below the low hump of a hill. Then two brighter lamps illuminated a dock, a jumble of masts, a long stone building with a sagging roof. Human shapes and a wisp of music.

Faustino was surprised when the dock drifted past them. "Aren't we stopping?"

"Not here," Prima said. "We land here, the whole place know our business in two minutes. We goin' on a little way."

She left him and went to the wheelhouse. A minute or two later, the boat swung toward the bank, Lucas revving the engine in quick bursts, then reversing it. *El Peregrino* drifted, then shuddered against something solid. The engine died; someone moved at the prow. Then Mateo, his face bluish in the moonlight, was standing beside the boat, looping rope around a wooden bollard.

From somewhere close to Faustino, Edson Bakula softly said, "This is what the locals call Dead Man's Landing. It's where they brought the bodies of people who died farther along the river. The graveyard is through these trees. That's why we're tying up here. People tend to avoid it at night. The power of superstition, as you might say. Now, I'd like you to sit quietly while we get a couple of things organized. You OK?"

Faustino stared incredulously at Bakula's black silhouette, then said, "Well, let me see. I've been kidnapped by a deranged tour guide, a teenage girl, and a bunch of bodybuilders. I've been taken on a river trip more tedious than anything I've ever known, and believe me, coming from a sportswriter, that's saying something. I've ended up at a graveyard at the butt end of nowhere in the pitch dark. I've got three cigarettes left. On the downside, the fried chicken could have done with a little less chili. But on the whole, pretty much the perfect vacation experience. How could I not be *OK*?"

Bakula said nothing for a couple of seconds. Then his arm moved and something blacker than the darkness fell onto Faustino's lap. A jacket of some sort, made of slithery synthetic material.

"Put this on."

"Thanks, but I'm not cold."

"No, but that shirt of yours is more or less luminous in moonlight. You could be seen a mile away. Lucas wanted to black up your face with used engine oil, but I decided that wouldn't be necessary so long as you wear the hood up."

"You're too kind."

The three brothers were silently busy at the locker.

Faustino saw that they too were now wearing dark hooded jackets. Something heavy clunked onto the deck: the sports bag, its Nike logo palely visible. Faustino heard it being unzipped. A disk of light appeared briefly on the boards. Mateo murmured something, passing things around. Then the sound of oiled metal sliding against metal, a sharp click. Then another. Moonlight reflected dully from something long and flat-sided protruding from Juan's hand.

Faustino stood up.

"Jesus Christ, Bakula. Are those guns? They're guns. What the hell is this?"

FIVE: TIME IS FOLDED LIKE CLOTH

The years passed. Time unfolded, but I could not see its pattern yet.

I woke with a start one night because something like a fever had flashed through me, beneath my skin, then vanished. I sat up and saw that the cabin was dimly lit by four small yellow flames. They burned like candles at the tips of Maco's fingers. With his other hand, he was lifting our tattered bedsheet, peeping up Blessing's legs.

I was glad to see him. At nightfall I had made a veneration, but he had not come.

When he saw me looking at him, he smiled his triangular pointed teeth at me and winked the eye in the red half of his face. He lowered the sheet, going *Hmm-hmmm*.

He said, "What did you want?"

I told him again of the troubles I was having with those of our people who would not submit to me because they wanted to believe in the white man's religion. That some of them were afraid to do Worship.

"You've done as I told you? Taught your people that the white religion is only a disguise for true Worship? That those white saints are bleached ancestors? That the Dreamer of Visions, San Juan, is really Oxufa, and that what's-her-name, Teresa, is Ochandja, and so on?"

"Yes," I said, "I have taught them so."

Maco's eyes glittered. "And you have told them that the white priests' hocus-pocus with the bread and the wine is really a veneration to me?"

"Yes," I said. "But I think some of them are looking through the mirror from the other side."

"What's that supposed to mean?" Maco said, snappish. "Don't use your *pai* riddles on me, man."

So I quickly covered my face with my hands and bowed my head; then I said, "I mean that some of our people are hiding their white religion behind Worship, not the other way around."

"So punish them," Maco said, scratching an armpit with his burning fingers.

I asked him, "How can I punish people who see their lives as punishment?"

He sucked his teeth. "Yes," he said, "that is always a tricky problem."

He closed his eyes. "I see that you are thinking about a sign."

I nodded. Maco pressed the tips of his candle fingers together, and a bolt of bright fire shot from them, up to the timber and leaf thatch of the cabin. A small green-and-yellow lizard shut down its eyes and scuttled to safety along a beam. The roof flamed and crackled. Maco clenched his hand and drew the fire back to himself.

"One like that?"

"Yes," I said. "That is what I was thinking."

Maco closed his eyes again. "I see the towers of your colonel's church are almost finished."

"Yes. A boat brought the bells up from San Juan yesterday."

He stood and stretched, yawning. "Very well," he said. "When those bells are up, I'll smite the church. I tell you what: I'll smite it twice. I'll wait till they start rebuilding and do it again. There shouldn't be any shilly-shallying after that. As long as you do your work."

I thanked him in the proper way. He waved his glowing hand, as if to say, It's nothing.

He said, "I must be going. I can't stand this place, anyway. Everywhere stinks like it's been sprayed by a tomcat, have you noticed?"

He leaned over the bed. "Nice wife. She'll never get fat like some of them. Pretty child too. Girl, is it?"

"My daughter, Achasha."

"Good name," Maco said, then glowed his eyes at me. "You owe me."

"I am your servant always," I said, fearful.

"Damn right," he said. "And you have no idea what 'always' means."

Smiling, he turned and walked through the wall. I saw that the face on the back of his head was weeping: a red tear ran down the black cheek; a black tear ran down the red.

What an end-of-world sound they made, those towers, when they fell. What a clamor of crashing brick and bell! And Maco's strike on them was like a fiery split in the dark sky. My vision burned green long after. And because when all came running, I was already there, standing at the edge of the rolling dust, there were murmurs, and doubters slid their eyes at me.

I thought that Maco had toppled the colonel too. For five days, he kept himself in his rooms and spoke to no one, not even me. But he was stubborn. A month later, he brought a priest upriver to hold a Mass in the wreck of the church. This was a feast day the whites call the Annunciation of the Virgin Mary, who is the impossible mother of their god. Which I had taught my people was the ancestor day of Amalu, who watches over births. The priest was the same fat sweating one who had married me to Blessing. The colonel made all his slaves except the ones in the faraway cane fields be there. We filled the space around the church like blackflies around a corpse. He did not see, as I did, that most had yellow threads around their wrists or ankles, or tiny smears of yellow pollen on their hands or feet. Amalu's color. I rejoiced, and later, when under the cover of the night I made a blood veneration to Maco, many watched me, silently.

It was the fire next time.

Maco smote the scaffolding around the new towers and blew on the flames until they seized the roof. Lead went molten and wept down the walls. He put his signature on his work; that church was a heart of red fire inside black ribs. And as he had said, there was no shilly-shallying after that. No question of *pai* or not *pai*. No looking wrongways through mirrors. I had brought my people back to themselves.

Or so I thought.

Fool.

Nothing is ever finished.

Ogun Rasa, the ancestor of health and sickness, is greedy for sacrifice. When the drying disease that the whites call cholera came the first time, I did not know this. The venerations I made were hasty and weak, and the offerings I made were poor. So he took Blessing and Achasha from me. The nearest he comes to kindness is quickness; so between my daughter's first purge and her last breath there was only a day and a night. And after another day and a night, with our dead child still in her arms, Blessing also died. At the end there was nothing I could do but brush the flies off them.

Their deaths seemed to satisfy Ogun Rasa. I came back from the graveyard with soil still on my hands, and he made me a healer. I went half ghostly among the cabins and the houses on the river and the sleep shacks in the cane fields;

many of those I nursed were spared. I raged inside myself that this was so, that I had not saved my wife and my daughter yet could save others. But my stature among the people grew. It grew like one tree that rises above the roof of the forest, with a thick vine named sorrow wrapped around its trunk.

When the cholera came back seven years later, I was better prepared.

From the half-wild boatmen who traded with the feathered Indians far upriver, I had bartered medicinal plants and learned their uses. Little by little I had taken from Ma Rosa and Ma Perla the knowledge they jealously guarded. Little by little I learned the ways of Ogun Rasa.

As soon as I could, after the news came of the first deaths among the riverside houses, I began to gather offerings to him. They were difficult to get, and I had much trouble. I believe that the colonel heard of what I was doing, but he did nothing to stop me. I took everything to my quiet place along the river beyond the graveyard. By then the cholera had gotten into the cabins, and the colonel had closed his house up and lit smoke fires to keep away the contagion that drifted in the air. Or so he believed.

Ogun Rasa took a long time to reach me. Perhaps the bitterness I felt toward him flavored my venerations. By the time he emerged from the trees, the moon was low in the sky and

169

I was almost exhausted. He stood tall above me, wearing the woven hat with the wooden brim, the long white veil that covered his face, the bloodstained robe that covered his sad, sore-encrusted body, leaning on the staff with the living snake wrapped around it. The stench that came off him mingled with the smell of burnt meat, and I had to take my breath in through my mouth not to vomit.

I made my submission to him, begging for his help, and when I had finished, he let out a sigh like a wind that had blown from some cold and desolate place. The snake unwound itself from the staff and slithered, tasting the air with its purple tongue, to where I knelt. Its coils were warm and dry, but when they wrapped around me, they left a coolness that spread peace through my blood. I fell into a dream of Blessing and Achasha in their full health and beauty, and when I awoke, the dawn was drowning the stars. I felt strong, and the memory of happiness had returned to me.

I was working on a child in one of the distant cabins when a frightened boy ran in. The colonel had sent for me. Cholera had gotten into the house and seized his sons.

I went in through the kitchens. The women there were crying. They had covered their mouths and noses with cloths. I asked them which of our people were sick. Two washing girls, they told me, and Benito, the half-wit. And Virginia, the maid who looked after the colonel's sons. I told them to boil water in covered pots, and when it had boiled, they must not uncover it or touch it. I thought of telling them that their masks were foolish, but I did not.

The house was hot and dark, and a sharp reek hung in the air. It stung my eyes. Climbing the stairs, I heard cries and groans, and they led me to the room where the boys lay. Outside the door, the colonel sat with his head in his hands on a small chair made of gold-painted wood.

I stood before him and said, "Señor?"

He looked up. The whites of his eyes were yellowish and threaded with blood. He got to his feet like a man who is a thousand years old.

"I cannot lose them," he said. "They are why I live."

I do not think I spoke. The colonel led me into the room. The curtains were drawn and lamps lit. Felipe and Luis lay on two beds close together. There were three housemaids with them, wide-eyed and fearful. A metal dish by the window was the source of the sharp smoke that hurt my eyes and almost covered the stink of sweat and sickness.

The white doctor who had come up from San Juan was standing watching the boys. Everything about him was thin: his hair, his fingers, his face. He wore lenses on his nose that made his eyes big like a bird that hunts at night.

The colonel said to him, "This man has successfully treated many cases of the cholera. I would like you to explain to him what you are doing for my sons."

The doctor looked up and past me, expecting to see someone else. Then his eyes came to rest on me.

"You mean this nigger?"

"Yes," the colonel said.

The doctor looked at me like some shit he'd trodden in.

He said, "Don Sebastian, I realize that you are distraught, but—"

"Tell him."

I heard the danger in the colonel's voice, but the doctor did not.

He pulled the lenses off his face and said, "He would not understand."

"Damn it! Tell him!"

The doctor could not speak to me. He spoke to the ceiling, to the sleeve of his shirt, to his spectacles, to the colonel, to his own foot—but not to me.

"Very well. Cholera is a disturbance of the bodily humors. It excites the hot, or choleric, humor. Which is why it is called cholera. It is spread by an invisible miasma that haunts damp and impure air. The church believes that this miasma is the result of sinful behavior, and for this reason it often occurs where there are large numbers of slaves. This may or may not be so; I am a man of science, not religion. What is certain is that the inhalation of the pernicious miasma inflames the lungs, as we can tell by the hot, foul, and weakened breath that is characteristic of the infected. The heat in the lungs heats and thickens the blood, and by this means the disease descends to the lower body, resulting in violent purging of the bowels and vomiting. As we have seen, Señor."

172

Felipe arched his back and called out, "Papa! Papa!"

The colonel kept his eyes fixed on the doctor.

"The only proven treatments for cholera are those I have undertaken. I am burning oil of eucalyptus and camphor to repel the poisonous atmosphere. Because like attracts like, I have applied poultices of ginger and pepper oil to the lower body to draw away the heat. That your sons' bodies have become cool and moist is evidence of the effectiveness of this procedure. I have applied leeches to your sons' temples and feet to reduce the thickening of the blood. To rebalance the humors, I am administering opium, calomel, capsicum, and spirits of rum."

Luis, the younger boy, had agonies in his legs; he thrashed and groaned. I knew from the color of his skin that he was further down the road to his dying, that he had been the first to start.

The colonel said, "Will they live?"

The doctor pulled his shirttail free of his breeches and wiped his glasses on it. "If God wills it. Not if I waste time talking to this black."

I left the room. After a while, the colonel came out and closed the door behind him.

He said, "Dr. Madureira is highly respected in San Juan. He is the bishop's personal physician."

I stayed silent, and this displeased him.

"Don't stand there like a black stump, damn you! Tell me what you are thinking."

"With respect, Señor, the man is a fool. Everything he is doing is the opposite of what is right. He will kill your sons."

The colonel made his hands into fists. I thought he was going to strike me. Instead he went suddenly slack, like a sail when the wind dies. He walked unsteadily past me and stopped at the end of the passageway in front of the portrait of his grandfather. It was a picture of a stern man wearing a sword and a great wig like a tumbling fall of white water, standing in front of a pretty wilderness with his foot on the neck of a dead jaguar.

The colonel held his hands together behind his back and straightened himself. He said, "I know that they are calling you Paracleto now. Pai Paracleto. It is not the name I gave you."

"No, Señor."

"It is blasphemous."

"It is only a name, Señor."

"No," he said. "It is a title."

He turned away from his ancestor and came back to me.

"Can you cure my sons?"

"I do not know. I cannot promise it. I treat everyone the same. Some die; most live. I do not have the doctor's words to explain things."

The colonel looked at the floor.

"The ones that live. They live because they believe in your . . . authority, don't they? I know why they call you *pai*. I know what it means. But Felipe and Luis, they do not have this . . . this respect. So I must ask you: without it, will your methods work?"

I did not know. I had no answer. All I could say was, "I believe all bodies are the same."

The colonel stared at me as if I had told him that stars are the laughter of children or that trees dance at night. Downstairs his tall clock chimed the hour.

Then he said, "We are in hell, so we might as well work with the devil."

He went into his sons' room. I waited. He came out with Madureira, whose face was like an angry dog's.

The doctor said, "Señor, it is widely known in San Juan that you tolerate certain heathenish activities on your estate. That is your affair, and I make no comment on it. But that you should entrust the lives of your children to nigger witchcraft is something on which I cannot remain silent. The insult to my skill is not the least of it. I understand that desperation has brought you to this reckless course of action. But desperation is the enemy of reason. I urge you to reconsider. We are white men, Señor. It is our privilege, and our duty, to be guided by science and reason. Not to be ensnared by the barbarous superstitions of an inferior species."

The colonel listened to this speech in polite silence. He stayed silent when it was over, and I thought he would change his mind.

"Duty." The colonel said it quietly, and as if it was a word he had not heard before. As if he was turning it in his hand, studying it.

Then he lifted his eyes to Madureira's face. If he had looked at me that way, I would have felt whipped.

"Your science, your skill, did not save my wife or my newborn daughter. On consideration, I would rather spare you the distress of supervising the deaths of the rest of my family. If you would care to wait downstairs, I will pay you your fee and make the necessary arrangements for your return to San Juan."

The doctor's mouth opened and closed like a fish drowning. Then he walked to the stairs.

The colonel watched him go. He said, "There goes what is left of my reputation. And a pox on it."

We went into the room, and I set down my satchel of cures on the table between the two beds. One of the three maids met my eyes. I knew her; her given name was Felicia. I asked the colonel to send the other two down to the kitchen to bring the boiled water. Then I pulled back the curtains and opened the window and threw the dish of stinking stuff out. It fell at the feet of Ogun Rasa, whose veiled face was lifted toward me.

I found the courage to ask the colonel to leave me alone with his sons. He looked at me with a thousand words in his head, but none could find his mouth.

When he had gone, I went to Luis and held his face in my hand and asked him if he wanted to die. Because he could not hear me at first, I had to ask him three times before I forced the answer out of him.

Then I said, "If you live, your brother will live. If you die, your brother will die. Do you understand?"

His eyes were sunk deep in his face and struggling.

"It depend on you," I told him.

The girls came back with the water, and then I sent them away.

"Papa," Luis said, "there is a darkie on my bed. A darkie." His voice was less than the wind in dry grass.

Felicia looked at me with sad rage in her eyes.

I brought out my cures and worked for two days and two nights.

In the middle of the first night, the colonel stumbled into the room with a glass in his hand and said, "If my sons die, you will wish you had died with them. If they live, I will give you anything you want."

They lived.

I named my price.

The colonel said, "A house for worship? You mean a church?"

"No, Señor. An ordinary house. A simple thing. Four walls and a roof. Somewhere I can go to worship in peace."

He hummed and grunted. The sea in his eyes was full of running shadows. I waited.

"Where?"

"Up along the river, Señor, a way past the graveyard. A piece of nothing between the river and the plantation."

He sighed and swung his legs out of the hammock.

"Show me," he said. "Fetch my boots."

We went alone. He made me walk ahead of him, and he slashed at the undergrowth with his cane and muttered curses at it. When we got there, he wiped his face with his neckcloth and looked around. He saw the ashes and bones of my sacrifice fire but said nothing about it.

"I know this place," he said. "Over there somewhere are good rocks to fish from. I came here sometimes with my father. While I fished, he watched the river with his gun. Once he shot an alligator, but it did not die. He used to say that the uglier things are, the longer they live, and the ugliest things live forever."

He looked up at the trees, squinting at the streams of light that fell through them. From not far off a bird called, harsh as stones grinding together.

"I never liked the damned place. Never felt easy here. It suits you, though, does it?"

"It has quietness, Señor."

"Hmm. Do you know how to build a house? Can you work wood?"

"I worked with my father making boats. When I was a boy."

"Did you? I didn't know that. But it's not the same thing. You'll need help."

The colonel lent me three field men and one of the carpenters from the mill, a giant named Baltasar. The work was harder and took much longer than I had pictured. Three weeks just to clear the ground and cut and trim the trees. We had to shape the trunks where they had fallen, turning them on branches laid on the ground. Without a saw pit, we had to work the big two-handled saw flatways, pulling the teeth into the wood. Our backs and shoulders hurt us all the time we did this.

At the end of every day, I stopped in the graveyard and told Blessing and Achasha how the work was going.

When at last the frame was built, we thatched the roof with two coverings of palm leaves, held fast by lines of thin branches pinned down by sharpened twists of green wood. Looking at it, I felt a sorrowful pain that made me dizzy. I was reminded of the house where I was born. The shadow of a memory, of a life, that was lost.

We had nothing for walls. There was little stone in or near the place. Baltasar said it would take months to cut enough planks and months to dry them. So we made mud bricks, and it was a hard and filthy labor.

To give the bricks strength and lightness, we mixed the mud with used litter from the floor of the animal pens. Coarse yellow grass, dried cane leaves, and the droppings of horses, cattle, and pigs. We brought it up to the clearing in great baskets on the backs of two mules; we arrived inside black clouds of flies. We had to chop it up small with a sharpened spade before mixing it with red soil and river water. When we had stirred it all into a foul brown porridge, we slopped it into the shaping frames that Baltasar had made and pressed it down with our hands. We did this work naked, to save our poor clothes.

At the end of each cruel day, we washed ourselves in the

river, but I thought we would never be free of the stink. The field men hated this work. Twice I had to frighten their souls to make them go on. More than once savage rain ruined the bricks, sluicing them from the frames.

When three of the walls were built, I washed carefully, put on my house clothes, and asked to speak to the colonel. There was something else that I wanted. It had grown in me, this want, like the fingers of plants that force apart little cracks in baked earth, and it had flowered.

In the storehouse on the river, there was a high and dusty stack of wooden crates. I knew what was inside them. One after another, layers of straw and some strange hairy cloth, and glass. Glass of the most beautiful colors, so that looking through it you might be looking through blood or the sky or green water or into the sun. The colonel had brought this glass halfway around the world for a window in his church. A window that was a picture. I also knew what this picture was meant to be, because I had seen it painted on paper pinned on the wall of his writing room. It was the ghost of the white man's god showing his wounds to the half-believer whose name was Tomas. The crates were gray and dusty because the colonel would never have his picture window.

"I hear the work on the hermitage is going well," the colonel said. That was what he had decided to call it. "I also hear that you are stealing manure from the pens. I imagine that is why you reek like the outhouse."

"I am sorry, Señor."

"For the theft, or for the stink?"

"Both, Señor."

"It doesn't matter." He stood and walked to the open window and clasped his hands behind his back. "Why did you want to speak to me?"

I told him. He kept his back to me, looking out. After a long minute, he lowered his head the way white people do and call it praying.

He said, "You ask too much."

I kept quiet.

"I paid more for one sheet of the blue glass than I paid for you."

There were things I might have said. But I did not have to. Young voices and laughter came in through the window. The colonel's sons on their ponies. Luis, the younger one, leading, looking back at Felipe and pointing. I remembered the gray-purple of their sick flesh, their watery leakages. How they had retreated so quickly from death when I gave their bodies what they needed. How I could have let them go out like candles.

The colonel lifted his head and watched them pass. He put his hand to the back of his neck and worked the narrow muscles there.

"Very well," he said, "damn you."

"Thank you, Señor."

I was at the door when he spoke again

I own you, or is it vice versa now?"

Because I did not know what it mean

He said, "Hurry up and finish it ar

back here. I need you."

Together, Baltasar and I made the window in the carpe...

shop next to the mill. We used only the smaller panes of

glass. Few of them were the same size, but Baltasar took

pleasure in the complication of the task, enjoyed making the

frame, using his beloved planes and drills and chisels.

I had time to study the glass closely. Some of the panes,

when I held them at a certain angle in the light, had faint rip-

ples and eddies in them. They were like thin slices of halted

water or smoke. There was no white glass, no black glass,

and I wondered why this was so.

When the frame was made, we fixed it between two of the

uprights and built the rest of the wall around it. Then we put

in the glass, a pane for each of the thirteen ancestors. I spoke

thirteen devotions. We went into the house and stood bathed

in light. When we moved, a rainbow passed its hand over us.

I told all this to Blessing and Achasha. Sorrowing, because

they had not seen it.

Yet another month passed before all was done. We had to

coat the walls inside and out with clay and smooth it. When

ry, we painted it with white limewash. We used long-
dled brushes to do this, but sometimes it splashed us.
Then we had to make haste to wash in a bucket of water
because it burned our skin.

At last, on a night of the full moon, I made my first Worship
in my house. On the little altar that Baltasar had made, I
arranged the things that I had hoarded and traded and gathered and stolen. Thirteen smooth white stones marked with
the signs of the ancestors, written with my blood. Twenty-
six white seashells, thirty-nine knuckle bones. Three wax
candles, a small dish of salt, an iron knife with a wooden
handle that I had carved myself. Fish for the ancestors
of the waters, meat for the ancestors of the land. And last
of all, my most treasured thing: the little tin box that had
inside two twists of hair: one from Blessing's head, one
from Achasha's.

I lit a small fire in a metal bowl and burned tobacco and
sweet tree gum. Then I sat and began.

And They came. They all came.

One afternoon, I was giving the colonel his shave. For many years I had been the only other person to enter his room, and the only person—except for his sons and grandchildren—allowed to touch him. I twisted the hot water out of the cloths and laid them on his face. I sharpened the razor.

The colonel said, "I went into the forest again this morning."

He had taken to doing so. I could picture him closed up in its green darkness, feeling it swarm in on him, shrinking him.

"You should not do it, Señor," I said.

"I need to conquer my horror of it. It is an insult to God that I loathe anything He has created."

I looked at his shrouded face. The colonel had two men who worked full-time in the graveyard, keeping the forest away from his dead. He feared especially the snaking vines that creep then swell. He knew they wanted to slither into the white tombs, prise open the coffins, squirm and thicken among the bones of his wife, the tiny bones of his daughter. It was not greed that drove him, year after year, to hack away and burn the forest, to replace it with his measured ranks of sugarcane.

"Fear is the root of worship," I said, lifting the cloths from his face.

He smiled a little. "If that is so," he said, "I am becoming saintly."

I worked perfumed oil into his white stubble, my fingers denting deep into his cheeks where he had lost teeth. I wiped my hands, tested the blade of the razor against my thumb, and went to stand behind him. In the mirror, his eyes met mine.

He said, "I wish I had built my church."

So I knew he was thinking of dying.

"It was struck, Señor. It was not your fault."

"It was struck twice," he said, so fierce that his face looked young. "Twice, and by bolts from heaven. The bishop said it was a judgment. He was a fool, but even fools are sometimes right."

Perhaps I should have given him some comfort. But all I said was, "It is a priest's work to say such things. To give meanings to accidents."

186

He looked at me in the glass for a long, long second. A little bit of time outside time.

"You wear a mask, Paracleto. You all do, all your people. I have lived my whole life among masks."

"Yes, Señor," I said.

He sighed and closed his eyes. With the tips of my fingers, I lifted his chin, then made my first smooth stroke with the razor, up over the skin of his throat to the ridge of the jawbone.

A few months later, four men carried the colonel's coffin to the tomb. His two sons; his secretary, Marquez; I was the fourth. The white priests could not hide their disgust, but the colonel had commanded it on his deathbed, and they were powerless to prevent it.

Beyond the railings of the graveyard, the forest watched our procession, flexing its fingers.

Later, after the funeral breakfast, I was called to the colonel's writing room. Don Felipe and his wife, Doña Celestina, stood waiting for me. He, in his black coat and breeches, his white wig, with his long sunburned nose, looked like a comical marionette. *La doña*, black-veiled, black-gloved, was a shadow among the room's other shadows.

Don Felipe said, "This is my father's dying gift to you, Paracleto."

He held out a piece of parchment, folded three times. I took it and opened it out. I recognized the writing of Marquez and the colonel's hooked and wandering signature.

"It is your manumission," Don Felipe said.

I did not know the word.

"Your freedom. This document declares that you are now a free man." He held out his hand. "I am very happy for you, Paracleto," he said.

I took his hand. It was the first time I had touched him since the cholera.

Doña Celestina spoke from behind the veil. "But we would like you to stay with us, if it is your wish. We value you very highly, as you know."

Oxufa the Revealer entered the room, disguised as a peddler carrying bolts of cloth. I could hear the skulls on his belt chattering beneath his cloak, smell his travels on his breath. Don Felipe and Doña Celestina did not see him. He grinned at me. There was a white worm inside each of his eyes.

"Look," he said.

He unfolded one of his fabrics, year by year. A blue muslin on which the pattern shifted like light on the sea. He hung it in the air and sliced it bottom to top with his iron shears, and when it parted, the room was alive. The leather bindings of the colonel's books bloomed gray flowers of mold, and their pages writhed with termites. The heavy curtains dissolved into tattered webs; the increase in light disturbed the bats that clustered among the branches of the chandelier. The floorboards buckled and sprang; vines and blind, grasping roots spread to the walls and seized the furniture. Orange gourds and thorny fruit ripened on the decaying velvet of the colonel's couch. Hummingbirds sucked nectar from the shameless orchids that displayed themselves on the colonel's bureau. Where Don Felipe and Doña Celestina had stood, there were now two piles of black and dusty rags. A fat rat clambered into an upturned wig and gave birth to a litter of bald and sightless young.

"Look," Oxufa said again, unfolding another of his fabrics, year by year: a jet-black silk with a crimson shimmer. He hung it in the air and cut it, and the room was filled with night. Outside, a great clamor of furious voices and the light of many burning torches. Then the window glass exploded inward and thick tongues of fire came in, and where they licked, all was split and charred and blackened. The walls wept tears of burning sap. The parchment in my hand burned away and fell as flakes of ash on which the words still glittered. My hand also burned but was not consumed; it was as if I wore a fiery glove. The room fell away, and the fire spread in all directions, springing up in the darkness like bright flowers, which quickly joined together to make a riotous garden of flame, and with every new growth, there was a tumult of voices.

Then, as quickly as it had grown, the fire shrank and retreated until it had gathered itself into a single pyre beneath a gallows. A human body hung in the pyre, shrunken and congealed like a roasted grasshopper. I shared its unbearable torment for a flicker of time; then I departed from it, as if I had stepped through a glass door. I found myself walking, grieving and invisible, among the roaring multitudes gathered around the scaffold.

"Look once more," Oxufa said, and unfolded a fabric, year by year: a material that glittered like shards of glass, hurting my eyes. It was strong; Oxufa grunted and complained, working the shears. When it parted, I could see nothing at first, although I knew that far behind me there was a great city of pale towers that touched the sky. Then, slowly, the darkness formed shapes and I knew where I was. I walked through the graveyard, looking but not searching, until I came to Blessing's grave. She was awake and gazed up at me, smiling. The white dress was high on her legs.

She lifted her arms to me and said, "Husband, you are young and handsome again. Come. Come down and lie with me."

I said, "I cannot. We will wake our daughter."

Blessing reached through the narrow wall of earth into the neighboring grave where Achasha lay with her thumb in her mouth. Her hand caressed the child's shoulder.

"She will not wake," she said.

"I have business to do," I told her.

Blessing closed her eyes and spoke sadly. "Ah, business. Forever work to do."

"The whites gave me my freedom," I said, "but it burned."

Blessing said nothing. Perhaps she was asleep.

I walked along the track. It was blue in the moonlight, and I had five shadows. My house did not look like my house. A boy sat alone inside it, holding a white globe without the world painted on it. Colored light played across his face. I reached out my hand to him and was puzzled to see that it was covered in blood.

"Perhaps you need more time," Don Felipe said. "To think about what you might do."

Oxufa was fussily refolding his cloths, mumbling and shaking his head. The seashells at the ends of his braids clattered.

"No, Señor, I do not need time. I will stay."

"We are very glad, Paracleto," Doña Celestina said. "You are a good and faithful servant."

Oxufa gathered up his bundles. He slapped me on the back and left the room, chuckling. I heard him whistling as he walked down the hall. As soon as I could, I set off after him. I thought I glimpsed him shouldering his way through the mourners in the salon, but by the time I'd reached the far door, he was gone.

Six: The Tethered Goat

Faustino paced the jetty at Dead Man's Landing. When Juan loomed in front of him, he said, "Want to tell me what's going on? Where's Bakula?"

"Edson got some business in the graveyard. It don' take long. When he get back, we move out."

From the end of the jetty, a path led into the cemetery through a gap in an overgrown line of railings. Just beyond that gap, a tall wooden cross stood at a slightly wrong angle, its ancient wood silvery where the moonlight struck. It had once been white; small obstinate flakes of paint still clung to it. Something on a chain or long necklace had been looped over its arms. Faustino saw a dark shape pass in front of the cross; Bakula had returned.

◆   ◆   ◆

Faustino was not fond of wandering through graveyards at night. He was inclined to believe that people who were fond of it had something wrong with them. The fact that he was being escorted by three very big men carrying guns might have made him less nervous, but somehow it did not. He was foolishly relieved when the low mounds and vine-choked tombs dissolved into undergrowth and then taller trees. He found himself on a track between two great walls of darkness. It was fairly wide; a brave or reckless driver could have taken a Jeep along it. Its surface was hard reddish earth, although there were deep fissures and corrugations in places where water had coursed across it. Faustino wondered what stubborn traffic kept the track open, why the forest that leaned over it, allowed it to be there.

They walked in silence, on the moon-shadowed side of the track, for half an hour. Bakula led them, walking with the unhurried confidence of a man in his own garden. Prima was just behind him; then Mateo, then Faustino. Juan and Lucas brought up the rear, walking side by side as if to block any attempt by Faustino to escape, although where they thought he might escape to, Faustino could not imagine.

The procession halted where, to the right of the path, the trees had been cut back. Faustino assumed that the resulting area of low scrub had once been a cultivated field. Brilliant stars spilled down onto it. The group gathered in the shadows on the other side of the track.

Bakula said, very quietly, "Paul, I don't want to handcuff you to Juan, as we did before. It would cramp his style. So I'm going to have to trust you. Stay close to me and Prima from now on, and try to be quiet. And please don't do anything foolish."

Faustino cocked an eyebrow. Too loudly he said, "Such as what? Try to hail a cab?" Then a hand clamped itself over his mouth. It smelled of fried banana and gun oil.

Two hundred yards farther on, the group halted again. Peering ahead, Faustino saw that the track gave onto a large open space randomly punctuated by solitary trees, low clumps of bushes, and a few single-story buildings that were no more than slabs of paleness in the moonlight. No lights showed.

Mateo now moved up to the front of the group. He took his gun from inside his jacket, then ran, stooping, off to the left toward a patch of absolute darkness, and disappeared. A second or two later, Bakula followed him. Faustino felt a small hand take his, heard Prima whisper, "Come on," then he too was running. He stopped when Prima stopped, and then a powerful arm pulled him down. He sat, gasping as quietly as he could, feeling the roughness of a stone wall against his back. Two large shadows, Juan and Lucas, loomed toward him and squatted next to Prima. Faustino felt his nerves wriggle electrically and his bladder contract. He wanted to laugh. Prima's hand tightened on his; he had been unaware that she was still holding it. He managed to steady his breathing. Someone — Mateo, perhaps — whispered "OK" and he felt, rather than saw, Juan and Lucas move past him.

He turned his face toward Prima, and before he asked the question, she murmured, "Lucas and Juan gone to assess the situation."

He marveled at her use of the phrase.

After a very long time that was probably no more than ten minutes, the brothers returned and held a hushed conference with Bakula and Mateo. At first it baffled Faustino, then it seriously frightened him.

"The boy's where you said he'd be. He look OK."

"Who's with him?"

"He's by hisself. Watchin' TV." A brief flash of white grin in the darkness.

"So where are the guys?"

"The house with the six on the door. Across from the ole cane press? They got the windows covered up, but we can hear 'em watchin' the soccer game too."

"Can't tell how many. Def'nitely two, but maybe more. Ain't nobody roamin' round outside, far as we can tell."

"We could keep 'em penned up in there, Edson. But I guess they got phones."

"The place got just a skinny back door. We could maybe get in there, hit 'em real quick before they got a chance to call somebody."

"No," Bakula said. "Too risky. Anyway, I need to have a conversation with them."

"Yeah. How we gonna work that?"

"Well, either we have to persuade them to come out and talk to us, or we have to get in there. I'm not prepared to sit here and wait."

Then Prima said, "I got an idea. Señor Paul, you by any chance got a notebook or somethin' like that on you?"

When Espirito Santo scored their second goal against DSJ—a soft tap-in from three yards—Paco "Two Wallets" Morales leaned back from the television set and cursed foully and elaborately. This was something he had been doing for the past thirty minutes, with only short pauses for drinking beer.

"Man," he said, "we're gettin' *wiped*. I dunno why I keep watchin'. I'm just depressin' myself."

The other man in the room, whose name was Diego Samuel, put down the paperback he was reading—a Yankee crime novel by Elmore Leonard—and regarded the back of his colleague's head. Not for the first time, he thought what a dumb hairstyle that was on a forty-year-old ex-cop. Trying to pass as a rap artist or something. Pathetic.

"Wallets," he said, "it never occur to you that you're part of the reason Deportivo is getting trashed? You know, like it might have somethin' to do with the fact we got their best player sittin' across the way like a zombie instead of out there on the field?"

Morales half turned his head. "Nah, man. You know what? I figure, long term, we're doin' da Silva a favor."

"Yeah? How's that, then?"

"We teachin' that fat bastard you can't have a team that's one genius an' a bunch of turkeys. He need to know that. Am I right, or am I right?"

Diego closed his tired eyes and nodded. That was almost the perfect Two Wallets statement. The guy had a sort of stupid genius for self-justification. That was why he'd gotten himself a paid-off early retirement rather than the jail sentence he so richly deserved.

"See?" Morales now said, gesturing at the screen with his beer can. "We kick off, three passes later, the ball's back with our goalkeeper. I mean, what the hell is that?"

"I guess you're right, Wallets," Diego said. "Maybe you should go into management."

He couldn't stand the guy. Ten days ago, he'd only disliked him. And, yeah, feared him, just a bit. But the best part of two weeks out in this godforsaken spooky dump with only him, mostly, for company — that had made the difference. The way, for instance, he would lift up out of the chair a bit and noisily break wind without any apology. You could come back into the room, and it would stink like a farm where all the cows had dysentery or something. And it had never been part of the deal that he, Diego, would do all the cooking. Well, not cooking, but putting the lousy canned and frozen food together. Still, better that way, maybe; he'd never seen Wallets wash his hands.

Think of the money, that was the only way.

One hundred and fifty thousand U.S. dollars.

Thinking about it was like a drug, an anesthetic, a drop into sweetness. As soon as Varga had said it, pronounced the figure, it had started to work. Three days, the captain had said, fifty thousand a day. Wow.

And he'd known, right away, what he'd do with it.

A couple of years back, he'd gone south, down to the islands. One of them, one of the small ones with no hotels or clubs or any of that crap, was Paradise. With a capital *P*. Palm trees leaning over white sand that was silver at night. No traffic, nothing. Nice laid-back people.

He'd got talking to an old hippie-type guy who ran a bar on the beach. The guy had said, "You know what? I love it here. But I gotta quit, one of these days soon. The thing is, I can live, OK, but I don't really make any money. I need to do this, do that, buy stuff, improve the place, you know? And I can't do it on what I make. I'm like just ticking over. You know what would be beautiful? If I didn't have to *depend* on it. If I had a stash of money put away somewhere, so I wasn't always thinking what the hell do I do if the going gets rough. You know what I mean? So I could just do this for *pleasure*."

So true.

And ever since Varga had pitched the scam to him, sitting in the cruiser up the far end of San Pedro, Diego had been dreaming, industriously. He wouldn't do the place up much. Keep it slightly rough, ethnic, the way the tourists on the boat trips like it. Driftwood furniture. Serve barbecue fish (a boat — he'd have a boat) and lobster, salad, cold beer, not much else. One of those quiet little Japanese generators to run the nice soft lights and the fridge and the music. A house out back behind the trees. A hammock. Yes.

Except it hadn't been three days. It had been fourteen, with this farting numbskull extortionist for company. Still. One hundred and fifty thousand dollars. God is good, but He makes you wait.

He checked his watch. An hour since the call from Varga saying that the da Silvas had quit fooling around and come up with the money. Diego was glad that they wouldn't, after all, have to cut off one of the kid's ears or some other piece of him. So only three, maybe four hours before he could get the hell out of here.

He kept going back and forth about Marcia and her kid, whether to take them with him down to the island. She'd love it, of course, cooking and running the joint. Wearing a bikini top and one of those sarong things, the gringo tourists looking at her. And the climate would be good for the kid's lungs. Get him swimming and all. Build him up, no more of those doctors' bills that are the price you pay for sleeping with his mama.

On the other hand, there was, well, freedom. Freedom from complication. From responsibility. And there are always plenty of girls.

And it was a girl's voice he now heard.

"Hola, Señor! Señor?"

He swung his feet off the table and grabbed the shotgun.

Wallets turned away from the TV.

"What?"

"Shuddup," Diego hissed.

"Hola, Señor! You at home?"

Wallets got up and pulled the Colt automatic from his shoulder holster and said, "Who the . . . ?"

"Wallets, for Chrissake."

Diego fumbled the table lamp off and pumped the gun. He went to the window and tweaked aside the sugar sack that they'd rigged for a curtain. Wallets went to the door and leaned beside it with the Colt up against his cheek.

The clear space in front of the house was awash with moonlight and there was a girl, a kid, standing in it.

She called again. "You in there, Señor?"

Diego looked at Wallets with a question on his face, and Wallets shook his fat head.

"Señor," the girl called again. She was starting to sound bored or uncertain. "Señor, if you in there, I got a message for you." Dragging out the last word: *yoo-oo.*

Before Diego could do anything about it, Wallets yelled through the door, "Who the hell are you?"

Diego watched the girl sort of cock her head.

"Ah, Señor. Good evenin'. I brung you a message."

Wallets looked over at Diego, whose face was coming and going in the glow from the television. "Who is it?"

"A girl. I dunno, man."

"See anyone else?"

"Nope."

"OK. Poke that damn cannon out the window an' keep watchin'. No, maybe you should slip out around the back. No, wait. Stay there."

"Jesus, Wallets, which?"

"Stay there," Wallets said, trying to sound professional, and he slipped the door chain along its slot and opened the door a crack.

"Who are you, girl?"

The girl said, "Me name Maria, from the village. I brung you a message."

Wallets moved around to the other side of the door so that he could see her.

"What message?"

"I dunno, Señor. Is written on this piece a paper. I dunno what it say." She held a hand up level with her face. There was something white in it.

"I think you should shoot her," Wallets said.

"Aw, man," Diego said. "No. Come on."

"Señor?"

Wallets looked heavy at Diego, then put his mouth to the opening again. "Who give it you?"

"Some guy. We was hangin' out down the dock an' this boat come in, an' the man say ten dollars for someone to come up here an' give this message to the man at house number six."

Wallets looked at Diego, and Diego looked at Wallets, and while they still didn't know what to do, Espirito Santo scored again.

"Shit," Wallets said. "You on your own, girl?"

"Yeah."

"How come? You ain't scared comin' up here by yusself?"

"Fuh ten dollars I ain't scared. I don' wanna stand here all night, though. You want this or not, man?"

"OK, girl, just you wait there a minute while I get my pants on."

To Diego he said, "What you think?"

"Hell, I dunno. Did Varga say anythin' about this?"

"No."

"Well, I don't like it," Diego said.

"Nor me. OK, lissen, here's what we do. You go out back, around the side, stay close to the wall, OK? Go 'round left, where the bushes is. I get the chick to give me the paper. Anythin', just anythin', don't look right to you, you blast off a coupla rounds an' get your ass back in here, right?"

"I dunno. Well, yeah, OK, I guess so." Diego took a deep breath and held the shotgun up against his chest. "Count to twenty before you get the girl to walk up, all right? And not too quick."

He went out through the kitchen and unlocked the door and pushed it open with the palm of his hand while he stayed against the wall with his backside against the warped worktop. When nothing bad happened, he went out. He heard the girl call, "Hey, Señor. You find them pants yet? C'mon, man, I ain't got all night. Jesus."

Prima saw a hand come out through the narrow gap in the door and make a clutching gesture. She heard the man's voice say, "OK, kid. Sorry to keep ya waitin'. Gimme the message an' get the hell outta here, OK?"

So she stepped up to the door and put the tightly folded page from Faustino's notebook into the man's hand. She saw flickering light on the metal of a gun and one eye.

She said, "You took your damn time, man," and then got out of the way.

Wallets pushed the door closed and one-handedly fumbled the piece of paper open, looking to read what was on it by the light from the television. He was trying to figure out why someone would pay ten dollars to deliver the single word Hello when he heard a muffled grunt from the direction of the doorway into the kitchen. He looked up and saw Diego standing there. He had a red-and-black-striped bandanna across his mouth and a big heavy-bladed knife against his throat. His eyes stood out of his face like two eggs. The man behind him was a huge dark shape with a hood, like a monk or something.

Wallets dropped the note and lifted the Colt; then the front door crashed inward onto his back. He fell, firing once into the floor, then lost his grip on the gun because a foot slammed down onto his arm. Something heavy, a body, came down on top of him and prevented him from moving. When he got free of it, he understood that he and Diego were lying on the floor and three large men were aiming guns at them.

He cried out, "Don' shoot! We're police officers!"

Mateo smiled down at him. "We know that, man," he said. "You think that gonna make us less likely to kill you?"

Faustino, aghast, had watched the proceedings from inside the shell of a house thirty yards away. When Prima walked back to where he and Bakula were crouching, she had said nothing at all. When Juan stepped into view and called, "It sorted, Edson," she said, "Thank you for the paper, Señor Paul. Like I said, it didn' make no diff'rence what was on it."

Faustino lit one of his cigarettes.

Faustino followed Bakula and the girl among the buildings, which, he now realized, were long-abandoned. What had seemed in that first moonlit survey a small village was actually a disorderly cluster of tumbledown bungalows and roofless sheds. Number six was, it seemed, the only habitable place. But now they approached another, much larger one. Like the others, its walls were concrete blocks coated with fractured and time-stained mortar. Unlike the others, it had several large glassless windows, some with their wooden shutters open. On the ground close to one of these openings, incongruously, a television satellite dish stood on a tripod, aimed at the moon.

When they were some twenty paces from this building, Bakula stopped and held a murmured conversation with Prima. She nodded, her face lowered. Bakula rested his hand briefly on her head. Faustino waited, standing a short distance away. He could not hear what was said. What he could hear, faintly, was a rising and falling sound like waves collapsing onto a beach. It was overlaid by a continuous excited babble. Soccer commentary.

A hand touched Faustino's shoulder, and he turned.

"Come," Bakula said. Prima stood beside him. She was trembling and holding her lower lip between her teeth.

The entrance was a pair of big doors, almost like those of a church. They were standing open. Stepping just inside, Faustino could see that the building had been erected around a much smaller, far more ancient structure. The irregular rectangles of moonlight and the single low-wattage lightbulb that illuminated the space made it difficult to make out clearly what it was, but gradually Faustino realized that he was looking at the skeleton of a small wooden house, or hut. Its uprights were stout, roughly hewn timbers. All manner of things had been fixed to them: scraps of paper, shapes of limbs and animals cut from tin, strings of beads, clay medallions, banknotes, ribbons, crutches. The place was some sort of shrine. The surviving rafters were thick tree branches stripped of their bark. Only part of one wall remained: a frail-looking screen of mud bricks. Somehow it supported a large window divided randomly into panels, some empty, others glazed with cracked stained glass.

More or less in the middle of this ruin was a single bed, iron-framed, with a mattress, a sheet, and a pillow. A young man sat on it watching a television set that stood on a wooden box; a long extension cable snaked away from it into the gloom. He was hugging a soccer ball that rested on his lap. The light from the screen wavered on his face.

"Rico," Prima said. It was scarcely more than a whisper, but the boy on the bed turned his face toward the doors. His expression was blank, as if he was aware of the presence of others but was unable to see them or make any connection between them and himself. After a moment or two, he turned back to the television.

The boy's mournful isolation had a surprising effect upon Faustino. It filled him with a kind of dread, a sense of desolation, as though this inexplicable captivity were happening to him. Or had, or would, happen to him. It was a horrible and intense empathy that made him want to cry out, to fall to his knees. He turned to Bakula and saw that the guide was studying him with cool, almost cruel, interest.

"So why doesn't he leave? Why doesn't he just walk away? There's nothing stopping him." Faustino's voice was harsh, angry.

It was Prima, not Bakula, who answered him. "Yeah, there is," she said, and pointed. "Look."

The floor surrounding the remains of the hut was smoothed concrete. On it, three feet or so inside the doors, a line of what looked like dried and crackled dark paint ran the width of the building. As far as Faustino could make out,

211

it continued unbroken around the other three sides. Inside this great rectangle was another continuous line of some whitish substance.

"Blood an' salt," Prima said.

"What?"

"Blood an' salt. Rico can't cross it. Not unless he want to be lost to hisself f'rever."

She squatted on her haunches and rested her chin on her hands, staring across at her brother the way you might gaze at a sad animal in a zoo.

Faustino glared down at her, then stepped across the two lines, turned, and stood with his arms out. Prima and Bakula watched him, expressionless. He stepped back over.

"Hey, Brujito! You see that? Come *on*, kid. Let's get out of here. It's over."

Prima sighed. "It no good. He can't hear you."

"Can't? Or won't?"

Prima was looking into the dim sepulchral space again. "Either. Both. Same thing. See, Señor Paul, that there's Rico but like gone. Like a flashlight or somethin' someone took the batt'ry out of, yah? It don't really matter 'bout them guys back there. Wasn't them stoppin' Rico leave."

She glanced up at Faustino uncertainly, then away again.

"Rico's spirit come from his ancestor called Achache. Achache sometime called the Magician, sometime the Dancer, on account of he's nimble and playful. It from him Rico get his skill at soccer. That why Rico not got a big head 'bout it, like some others. But now Rico think Achache have left him. Been taken from him. An' the only reason why that happen is Maco is angry with him. Have punish him."

"How do you know this, Prima?"

"Look what in front of your eyes. You got some other way to explain this?"

Faustino did not, and realizing it suddenly made him very tired. He felt himself slump inside, felt something within him give up.

"OK," he said. "So why? Why does he think Maco is angry with him?"

"I dunno. Someone must of persuade him. I dunno how. Rico can't of done nothin'."

"Who could have persuaded him? Someone in the police?"

She shook her head. "Nah. They wouldn' know how."

"So who would? Who could do that?"

Prima looked down at the ground. She muttered something.

"What?"

"Paracleto," Bakula said.

Faustino spun around, startled. He had almost forgotten the guide was there. He was leaning in the doorway with his arms folded.

"Paracleto," he said again. "That's why, we think, Rico came here, to this particular place. And he cannot leave until Paracleto returns. To intervene with Maco on his behalf.

To allow his estranged spirit to cross these barriers that you find so unimpressive, and reenter his body."

"Jesus Christ," Faustino muttered. He fished his crumpled cigarette pack from his pocket.

"Not in here, Paul."

"What?"

"Please step outside if you want to smoke." Bakula softened his tone and gestured apologetically toward the wooden husk of the shrine. "It's a bit of a fire hazard."

Faustino exhaled a blue cloud. The moon was directly above them now, and smaller, but intensely bright. He and Bakula stood on their small and sharply defined shadows.

"OK. So what happens now?"

"We wait. I'm afraid Ricardo will have to remain the tethered goat until the tiger arrives."

"And when might that be?"

"I don't know. Let's go and see if we can find out."

The sugarcane press was a fairly simple device. It was taller than a man and built of heavy hardwood timbers that were old, weathered, split in places, and grayish in the moonlight. In the middle of a square frame, a column like a massive screw passed between two thick wooden plates. The lower plate was a slab above a trough into which the juice from the crushed cane once ran. The upper plate was driven down the screw onto the cane by revolving two long wooden arms, bent poles. They would have been turned by a pair of oxen; in the absence of such beasts, Lucas and Juan stood ready to do the job. It seemed to Faustino that they were the ideal substitutes.

Two Wallets Morales and Diego Samuel were brought over to the press. They both had their wrists bound in front of them with heavy gray duct tape, and another swipe of the same stuff across their mouths. Their pants were down around their ankles so that they had to shuffle along. Mateo urged them along, poking them with his gun now and again, clucking his tongue like a man rounding up chickens.

When they were close to the press, Mateo told them to stop and said to Bakula, who was standing in the moonlight with his hands in his pockets, "Which one you wanna do, Edson?"

Bakula looked up. "The one with the stupid hair."

"OK," Mateo said. He tapped Diego on the top of his head with the gun. "On your knees, man."

Diego knelt.

"You," Mateo said into Wallets' ear. "Over here. C'mon, now."

One of Wallets' eyes, the right one, was puffed up; it looked like the buttocks of a sleeping piglet. The other one was wide and full of terror. Mateo forced him into a kneeling position with his head on the lower plate of the cane press: the posture of a French aristocrat at the guillotine.

Bakula nodded.

Juan and Lucas leaned stiff-armed against the handles of the press, grunting and going, "Whew, hey, how long since someone use this thing?"

They moved forward, pushing, starting to circle. The timbers groaned, then squealed. The upper plate came down, reluctantly at first, then more easily. When it touched the top of Morales's head, he twisted so that the right side of his face was against the lower plate and his one good eye was looking straight at Diego Samuel. The upper plate continued to descend, pressing his left ear into his skull. He managed to make a faint sound.

Faustino looked away. Beside him, Prima was an intent black shape. Only her eyes were distinct, and they were focused on Bakula.

The creaking stopped.

Lucas said, "Hold on there, bro. Let me ease me shoulder. Damn, this thing stiff."

Juan also let go and straightened. "Yeah," he said. "Edson, it OK we take a short break? Reckon the next bit gonna be the hardest."

"You're right," Bakula said.

Mateo went over to Diego and ripped the duct tape off his face. Faustino winced at the sound it made coming away from the skin.

Diego inhaled gasps, moving his head from side to side. When he could speak, he said, "You bastards. What the hell're you doing? What's this for?"

Mateo jabbed his gun into the top of Diego's head and said, "What you think we doin', mister kidnapper policeman? We squeezin' information outta you."

Diego lifted his head up against the pressure of Mateo's gun and let out something like a sob; it was among the saddest sounds that Faustino had ever heard.

"What you expect the man to say? You still got his mouth taped, you sick mothers."

Mateo sighed like a deeply disappointed man. He said gently, patiently, "It ain't difficult, man. We don' *want* your ugly friend there to talk. We want *you* to talk. But we figure that once you seen the way his head pop, you gonna be much more cooperative, know what I mean? 'Cause you seen how unpleasant it is. Thought about havin' the same thing done to you."

Diego stared back at him.

Juan said, "How that shoulder, bro? You ready for the last heave?"

Lucas said, "Yeah, I reckon. C'mon, then. Let's get it done."

He leaned against the pole, and it inched forward. Morales' legs shot out backward, and his toes pressed the ground, raising his body. His slack belly sagged.

Diego yelled, "OK! OK! Jesus! What? What, damn you?"

Bakula stepped closer and looked down at him. "What we would like to know," he said, "is when the man you call Paracleto might come here. Do you know that?"

"Yeah," Diego said. "Sometime around midnight."

"What, tonight?"

"Yeah."

Mateo said, "Well, I'll be damn. Look like you got the timin' right on the button, Edson."

"Tell me how you know this," Bakula said.

Diego shook his head sadly. He looked like a man seeing Paradise fade into the distance. "Wallets got a phone call."

"Wallets?"

"The guy you're killin' over there."

"All right," Bakula said. "And?"

"The man said da Silva finally stopped stallin' and came up with the money. Late this afternoon. So tonight Paracleto's comin' up here to do his hocus-pocus thing on the kid."

"What man? Who do you mean, 'the man'?"

Faustino said from the shadows, "Eduardo Varga."

There was a silence during which Bakula gave Faustino an interested look.

"Yeah," Diego said. "Varga. All right, then. What else don't you sonsabitches know?"

"Will Paracleto come alone or with others?"

"I dunno." Mateo pushed the gun harder against Diego's scalp. "I don' *know*, man. Last time he came, he had two guys with him, but—"

"Who were these men? Colleagues of yours?"

"Couldn't tell you. They had these crazy-like hoods on, you know?"

Bakula looked at Diego for a few seconds in silence, then nodded. "OK. So, when Paracleto's done whatever he's supposed to do, what happens to the kid? To Brujito?"

"I dunno."

Mateo let out a hiss of exasperation. "All this joker ever say is 'I dunno.' We wastin' time, Edson. Wan' me to shoot him?"

"No, lissen," Diego pleaded. "Lissen, man. I'm tellin'

you God's truth. Varga didn' say nothin' about that. Our orders is, we keep lookout here while Paracleto's in with the kid. When he's done, we split. Me and Wallets. Go on down to our boat, get back to San Juan, collect our cut. That's it. Job done. I'm not shittin' you, man. He didn't say nothin' about takin' the kid with us."

"So you leave him here. With whoever turns up tonight."

"Yeah. I guess."

Faustino felt Prima nudge his arm.

"I told you so," she said quietly.

He didn't reply. He was horribly fascinated by Two Wallets' weakening efforts to keep his body high enough off the ground so that his neck wouldn't break.

Lucas broke the silence. "All done, Edson? Wan' us to carry on?"

Without looking around, Bakula said, "Yes, carry on."

Lucas grinned, a white crescent of teeth. "Aye-aye, Cap'n." He took hold of one of the winding poles. "You ready, brother 'postle?"

"Guess so," Juan said.

"Oh God, no," Faustino murmured, and turned away.

Wallets' toes scrabbled for more purchase on the earth.

Grotesquely, Lucas began a sort of work chant, "Hey-yo, hey!" and leaned forward. Then, chuckling, he and Juan stooped under their poles and shoved in the reverse direction. The timbers moaned and mewled, and the plate rose reluctantly. Wallets brought his knees forward, very slowly, but did not lift his head from the slab. He had both eyes closed now, and he exhaled through his nose in a bubbly hiss.

Bakula had been standing with his hands in his pockets, staring into the night. Now he turned and said, "All right. Rehearsal time."

Shortly before eleven thirty, Bakula, Prima, and Faustino returned to the building that housed the shrine. They did not go to the double doors at the front; instead they went around to the back, where a single door with a lock but no handle was set into the wall. Bakula shone his flashlight along the concrete lintel and reached up. When he brought his hand down, it was holding a key. He unlocked the door and pushed it open.

"Come in."

Faustino followed Prima into complete darkness. He heard the door close behind him, and then a light clicked on. It was not a bright light, but his eyes flinched.

The room was the width of the building but only some four paces deep. It contained a good deal of stuff and a stale religious odor that took Faustino back, briefly, to the unbearable Sunday mornings of his childhood. Arranged haphazardly along the walls were items of furniture: a few simple wooden chairs, a chest of drawers, a cupboard with a small padlock, boxes of various sizes, an unplugged and rusty fridge. On a low table stood a number of African-looking carved figures, some naked, some dressed in clothes whose bright colors had faded. Other more naturalistic statuettes made of plaster were, Faustino supposed, Christian saints. Some, not all, had their faces painted black. On the long wall facing the entrance was another door, fastened with a hefty sliding bolt, and a small curtained window.

Speaking quietly, Bakula said, "This is what I suppose you'd call the vestry. I'm sorry it's not more comfortable. With any luck you won't have long to wait."

He went to the window. "Come over here, Paul. Prima, please turn the light off."

The room returned to darkness, and Bakula drew back the curtain. When Faustino's eyes had adjusted themselves, he found that he had a commanding view of the shrine. He looked down on it slightly; it seemed that the floor of the vestry was a little higher than that of the rest of the building. The double doors at the far end and the window shutters were still open; Faustino could make out the lines of blood and salt bisecting the angled patches of moonlight. The bare lightbulb still cast its weak and sickly glow over El Brujito, who was lying on the bed with his knees pulled up to his chest, perhaps asleep. The television set had been turned off.

"I want you to see what happens," Bakula murmured,

223

"and we think this is the safest, the best, place for you. You will be invisible to anyone in the building as long as you keep the light off. I'll leave the flashlight with Prima, but she will only use it if it's absolutely necessary. You must be completely silent, of course."

"No cheering, then."

"Not until it's over. And maybe not even then."

Bakula pulled the curtain closed, and Prima switched the light on. Bakula handed her the flashlight and the key to the outside door. Then he laid his hand on her head and looked into her eyes.

"I'm OK," she said.

"Yes. Lock the door behind me."

Then he left them. A click, darkness again, and the sound of the door opening and closing.

The three figures that emerged from the dense shadow of the track at eight minutes past midnight might have been returning from some ghoulish carnival. Two were similarly dressed. Over their pants they both wore a kind of kilt made of dangling lengths of coarse knotted string. At the ends of these strings were shells and small bones that chinked and clacked together. Both men — if that was what they were — wore red-and-black-quartered soccer jerseys and black hoods that rose to stiffened peaks almost three feet above their heads. The mouth and eyeholes were outlined with white paint. Hood One held a large seashell, a conch, in his right hand. Hood Two carried a small iron plate attached to a leather thong looped over his fingers. Both had satchels made of painted sackcloth slung over their shoulders.

The third character walked a couple of paces behind the others, and something in the way he moved suggested that he was an older man. He was barefoot and plainly dressed in white pants and a loose white shirt. His eyes and nose were concealed by a molded plastic mask, also white. His pale straw hat was frayed at the brim, and its band was adorned with small clay skulls painted red and black. In his hand he held some sort of wand or club: a bundle of thin canes bound together with embroidered bands of cloth. From the end of it protruded a small two-headed ax. He too carried a painted sackcloth satchel.

Diego stood outside house number six and watched this weird threesome approach. He had his back to the window and the empty shotgun cradled in one arm. If he'd leaned back a little, he'd have felt the muzzle of Juan's gun pressing into the base of his skull through the sugar sack curtain. He glanced over to see how Wallets was holding up. He looked more or less OK; he was leaning against the frame of the open door, the damaged side of his face in shadow. But Diego knew that if Wallets were to turn his head to the left, he'd be looking straight down the snout of the big Glock nine-millimeter pistol belonging to the guy named Lucas. And over in the shadow of the cane press was the third guy, Mateo.

Hood One called out, and Diego cautiously raised a hand in greeting.

"Yo, man. Everythin' cool?"

"Yeah," Diego said. "How long you reckon you'll be?"

"Long as it takes. Why, you in a hurry?" A flash of teeth in the mouth hole. "Don' tell me you ain't enjoyin' your little all-expenses-paid vacation up here."

Wallets cleared his throat and spat. "It sucks."

The man in the white clothes murmured something.

Hood Two said, "The *pai* here want to know how the superstar is."

"Same as ever," Diego said. "I checked him a half hour ago, looked like he was asleep."

"OK. Don't you guys go cuttin' off till we get back, now."

"We ain't goin' nowhere," Wallets said sourly.

"Right," Hood One said. "Let's get to it."

He raised the conch to his mouth and blew into it. A low and mournful sound unfurled itself from the shell. As it faded, Hood Two struck the iron plate with a wooden stick, producing a flurry of beats that settled into a slow marching rhythm. The conch moaned again, and to this unearthly music the strange trio walked toward the shrine.

Lucas murmured, "Nice work, guys. Now come inside an' relax."

When the sound reached Faustino, it sent a tickle of fear across his scalp. He got up from the chair. A pool of light appeared at his feet. When they were beside the window, Prima clicked off the flashlight and drew back the curtain.

It seemed that El Brujito had also heard. He sat up slowly and swung his legs off the bed; then, as the eerie rhythm grew louder, he stood, his back to the doors.

Faustino could not stifle a soft exclamation when the three freakish figures appeared in the doorway and stood silhouetted against the moonlight. As he watched, the hooded figure on the left drummed a fast pattern on the iron plate, then paused and repeated it. When the metallic echoes had died, the other man lifted the conch to his mouth. The sound it gave out was far louder than its earlier calls; it reverberated in the dark space like the cry of some huge and primitive animal facing its own extinction. The boy standing alone in the shrine swayed but did not look around. When the silence returned, it seemed denser than ever.

Now the hooded men moved into the building, shells clinking against bones. When they reached the barriers of blood and salt, they stopped. They were perhaps six feet apart. Each took a candle from his satchel and placed it between the blood and salt, careful not to touch either. Each lit his candle with a cigarette lighter, then stood and spoke a phrase in a language that Faustino did not know. Their actions were almost perfectly synchronized, as if in response to unheard commands.

They repeated this ritual at intervals as they worked their

way across and then down opposite sides of the blood-and-salt rectangle. When they were almost level with Brujito, the hooded man on the right stumbled slightly; his foot had encountered the television cord.

"Shit," he said, softly but audibly. He stooped and pulled the cable free of the wall socket with a single savage tug. Then he resumed his steady and stately progress along the blood and the salt.

When the fourth side of the rectangle had been lit by candles, the hooded figures stood just outside it, their backs toward the window behind which Faustino and Prima were concealed. Faustino saw that both men's jerseys bore the name BRUJITO above the number 10.

While this lengthy procedure had been taking place, Ricardo had grown increasingly anxious and restless. He had struggled to keep his hands still, baring his teeth with the effort. It seemed to Faustino that he was fighting the urge to run on the spot like a substitute waiting to come onto the field during a fraught passage of play.

By contrast, the masked man in the white clothes had remained motionless throughout, standing slightly stooped just inside the doors. Now at last he moved. He reached into his satchel and put something in his mouth. The flare of a lighter lit up his half-human face. Blowing cigar smoke in long plumes to the left and right, he walked slowly forward, extended his ax-headed club in front of him, and stepped

228

over the blood and the salt. As he did so, the conch sounded again, a low hoarse greeting that rose in pitch then fell away.

When the *pai* reached the skeletal timbers of the shrine itself, he stopped. Again he raised the club in front of him; then he called out a phrase, a sequence of unintelligible words. His voice was strong but rough-edged, as though long unused. The two hooded men called a reply, then repeated it; it became a slow chant, which they accompanied with claps and stomps, setting up a strangely off-kilter rhythm, a crippled waltz. The *pai* now stepped through the wooden pillars and began an unhurried patrol of the shrine. At ten different places he paused, uttered an incantation, and blew jets of smoke toward the surrounding darkness.

Ricardo now looked deeply agitated. His eyes were closed, and he moved his head in slow circles like someone easing a stiff neck. His body twitched, and with each spasm he would grimace as though enduring great pain or terrible joy.

Prima was gasping audibly; when a muffled sob broke from her, Faustino reached across and took her hand in his. To his surprise this quieted her.

The *pai* now handed the remains of his cigar and the ax club to one of the hooded men and added his voice to the chant. He approached Ricardo and stood facing him for a second or two; then he raised his right arm and laid his hand on the boy's head, palm on his forehead, fingers spread on his scalp.

The effect upon Ricardo was immediate. The palpitations ceased. His body went slack, like a suspended marionette, then folded as he sank to his knees. The *pai* stooped, as though effortlessly forcing the boy to the ground.

And then everything stopped. The chanting came to a shocked and shocking halt because the television set had turned itself on.

The screen was, at first, a brilliant writhing mass of spermy shapes; the white noise that hissed into the shrine might have been the sound of their swarming. Then fragmented bands of color began to scroll down the screen, accelerating into a rapid mesmeric flicker. At the same time, the white noise broke up into a fast sequence of different sounds — smeared snatches of music, babbled talk in a multiplicity of languages, electronic warbles — as if the set were searching frantically for a lost channel.

One of the hooded men yelled an obscenity; the other, muttering, "Jesus, Jesus," groped in his satchel and pulled out a gun, a heavy executioner's pistol with a stubby barrel. He inched sideways, peering into the shadows beyond the shrine, trying to remember where exactly he'd ripped the television cord from the wall.

The *pai* straightened up, his mouth gaping below his mask. Ricardo didn't move; he remained on his knees, his head close to the floor. Maybe he thought that what he was hearing was part of the process.

The screen resolved itself into two unsteady vertical bands, red on the left, black on the right. The soundtrack faded, then returned as a series of short fuzzy outbursts of speech. They sounded to Faustino like the rantings of a drunken madman roaming the streets at night, proclaiming his rage in a language of his own devising. Ricardo now lifted his head. He looked puzzled, like a dog dimly recognizing the voice of a previous owner.

Two pale shapes appeared on the screen, one in the red half, one in the black. In a wrenching moment of focus, they became eyes. In huge close-up. Pupils that contained points of fire. Corneas mapped with wormlike threads of blood.

Faustino's breath was locked in his chest. Prima's grip on his hand was fierce.

The eyes receded, and a complete face filled the screen. The red and the black were not paint, nor were they a mask. They were flesh; muscles moved beneath the skin as the broken, guttural voice rattled the television's speakers. The head and the mouth moved jerkily, out of sync with the sound, like a badly edited film. The mouth was full of yellowish, triangular pointed teeth. The words that came from it were incomprehensible to Faustino but not, it seemed, to the *pai*. He crept backward away from the television, trying to shrink himself. Behind him, the hooded figures had moved closer together. The one with the gun was pointing it aimlessly from place to place. The other had picked up the ax club; he clutched it tightly with both hands, staring at the television.

The eyes in the monstrous face moved slowly from side to side, as if the screen were a window and they were looking through it, seeking some guilty thing that was trying to conceal itself. A second voice now rumbled from the speakers, breaking into and overlapping the first. The head turned, revealing a second face where the back of the skull should have been. Both mouths were speaking. The volume rose to an almost unbearable level, distorting badly, but Faustino could make out scraps of words and phrases spoken in his own language.

"*Who calls Maco? Can't stand this damn place . . . stinks of tomcat . . . lies . . . All this way . . . Who is this? . . . cleto? Where? Not here . . . Tear . . . soul and heart out . . .*"

The masked *pai* was on his knees. He had removed his hat and covered his face with it. His body rocked back and forth in an ecstasy of terror. Ricardo had risen to his feet and was facing the screen. He held his arms out from his sides, his hands open: a shy, uncertain gesture of greeting.

As though some invisible hand had adjusted the volume, the roaring babble died away, fading into a single soft exclamation: "*Aaah.*" Maco turned; his first face filled the screen again. Then he closed his eyes and the image froze.

The ensuing silence had weight and density, like water. All that disturbed it was the *pai*'s muffled whimpering. Then the candles and the overhead light went out.

Faustino had not heard thunder; perhaps it had been drowned out by the continuous sound blast from the television set. So the lightning was unheralded, and it must have struck the earth just outside. In the nanosecond before his eyes recoiled, Faustino glimpsed the open ground and trees outside the doors. The flash had drained them of color; they were shapes scratched onto silver foil. Brutal beams of floodlight strobed the shrine, then withdrew. In the greenish darkness, someone cried out. Even before the sound had died, a second bomb of light silently exploded. The annihilating glare that filled the building robbed everything in it of solidity. The timbers of the shrine were as thin and delicate as burnt matches; the four paralyzed human figures were frail columns of ash inside a furnace.

Before he went blind, Faustino saw or hallucinated a group of figures in the doorway: a huddle of black-cowled monks gathered around a pale form, a wraith. Its afterimage, a reddish-purple negative, burned on his retina. He was still trying to blink it away when he heard Prima's whisper.

"Now he come."

Her nails were digging into Faustino's palms. He was trembling and his mouth was dry.

Now the only light was the dull red glow from the television screen. Maco's grotesque face was still placid, his eyes still closed. The hooded men were jabbering.

"Man, man."

"The hell with this, man."

"See anything?"

"Can't see any damn thing."

"Oh shit, man. I'm out of here, me . . ."

The candles relit themselves.

It seemed to Faustino that they were considerably brighter than before. Each flame was an unwavering spearhead radiating spokes of light. They illuminated the figure standing silent and motionless halfway between the salt-and-blood barrier and the framework of the shrine.

It was Bakula, but transformed. Like the masked *pai*, he was dressed in white. The shirt had a large floppy collar and wide, loose sleeves buttoned at the wrist. The pants were short, the legs fastened with cords just below the knee. He was barefoot. A line of black ran down his left cheek, a line of red down the right. He resembled, Faustino thought, a character from some piratical adventure.

The hooded men saw him no more than a heartbeat later. The one with the club yelped like a dog; the other swore and raised his gun, stepping sideways to get a clear shot at Bakula between the timbers of the shrine. But the gunshot that broke the air apart came from somewhere else. A lumpy spurt of blood erupted from the gunman's back, ripping open the letter T in BRUJITO. The impact of the bullet turned him slightly and threw him back against the wall. He slid down it, leaving a wide red streak on the powdery white paint. His right knee lifted, not much, and then the leg straightened and was still.

His companion had already dropped the club and lifted his hands high in the air; he swiveled from side to side in urgent confusion, unable to tell from where the shot had come.

"No, man. Don't shoot me, man. I ain't got a gun. Jesus! Don't shoot!"

A shadow moved behind the remains of the stained-glass window, and Lucas came into the light, clasping his gun in both hands out in front of him. On the other side of the room, another shape hulked beyond the candles. Mateo. Or Juan.

"OK," Lucas said. "Now you do everythin' I tell you, an' do it real slow, all right?" He spoke in a friendly and reasonable way, like a patient man giving instructions to a half-wit. "Let's see who you are. Take that damn fool hood off. Slow, remember?"

He was young, no more than twenty, with his hair shaved back to a narrow strip at the top of his head. Medium-dark skin slick with sweat. Mouth open, trying to draw breath in deep enough to smother his panic.

"Mmm . . . you less scary now," Lucas observed, tipping his head slightly to one side. "Not that you was that scary before. Now, you toss that bag thing over near to me."

The man's satchel landed, with a soft flump, between two

236

candles. Lucas investigated it with the sole of his foot before kicking it away.

"Lissen, man, I wasn't—"

"Hush up," Lucas said. "We got no time for lissenin', not to you. The man waitin'. Now, you lie down on your belly right where you are an' clap your hands 'top a your head. Good. That's right. You stay like that an' who knows, you might live through the night. You clear 'bout that?"

Bakula walked through the shrine toward Ricardo. On the television screen, Maco opened his eyes and watched him pass. There was nothing slack or submissive about the boy's posture now. It was almost comical, the way he held himself: stiff and expectant, like a military cadet awaiting inspection. The two stood face-to-face for a moment, then Ricardo went down on one knee.

"*Pai,*" he said, very quietly.

Bakula laid his right hand on Ricardo's head and held it there briefly. Then he murmured something and the boy arose. Bakula put a hand on either side of Ricardo's face and spoke again. Ricardo nodded; his body relaxed.

Bakula moved past him and approached the man in the white mask.

Fear had dehumanized the false priest. Kneeling, hugging himself, teeth bared, moaning, with half a face, he looked like a caricature from a church fresco painted to remind the sinful of the horrors of hell. A dead man wrenched from the grave on Judgment Day.

"I know who you are," Bakula said. It was not Bakula's voice. "You are a liar, a twisted mirror, a thief, an impostor. You wormed your way into this boy's trust in order to betray him. Worst of all, you have fouled my house and wiped your ass with my name."

The man's head twisted from side to side as if it were trying to untether itself from its neck.

"Yes, I know who you are. Your mask hides nothing. Do you know who I am?"

"Yes. Yes, yes, yes. Oh, Jesus and Mary." They were sobs, rather than words.

"And did you think, fool, that I would allow this? This abuse, in this place?"

"Please. My wife . . . my wife is sick. My son . . . It was the money. I needed—"

"Money?" The voice was full of a cold and ancient rage. "I was stolen. I was bought and sold. And you dare to speak to me of *money,* to offer that as an excuse?"

"I am sorry, Pai. I didn't know . . . I didn't believe . . . For pity's sake, forgive me. Please forgive me."

"I cannot," Bakula said, quite calm again. "I don't have the right. Forgiveness is beyond me. And there is too much to forgive, and not enough time. I have been sent to cleanse."

He reached into his pocket, took out a white cord knotted halfway along its length, and looped one end of it twice around his fingers. The masked man crawled backward, gibbering, begging, until he collided with the wall; then he scrambled to his feet and lurched away sideways, out of Faustino's line of sight. Bakula followed him, unhurried, implacable. There was a frenzied tugging at the vestry door, the bolt rattling. Faustino's heart stumbled; then, a moment later, he could not suppress a cry of alarm because the man's face had appeared at the window. The mouth was a wet red hole studded with stained teeth. The yellowish eyes rolled wildly behind the mask, hopelessly seeking hope within the darkness beyond the glass. His hands appeared, and it seemed that he might try to smash his way through.

Faustino recoiled, staggering into Prima. He felt both her hands grip his arm, perhaps to steady him, perhaps to save herself from falling. Faustino could not tear his gaze away. He saw Bakula's face, expressionless, distant-eyed, appear behind the false *pai*'s; he saw the white cord flick over the man's head, the knot lodge beneath the bulge in the throat and sink in; he saw the fingers' fumbling dance along the garrote. He heard the dry gargle, and then the face sank from view. Bakula's lowered head and straining shoulders followed it down.

A moment's silence, then feet drumming madly against the wall, then nothing.

"Oh, dear God," Faustino said hoarsely. His legs were about to fail him. He turned away from the window, groping for support. His knees struck something; it hurt. A chair.

He clutched it. He was breathing too fast but could do nothing about it. The faint beams of candlelight entering from the window illuminated grimacing idols and sorrowing saints.

"Prima? Prima, unlock the door, please. I have to get out."

The girl did not reply, and for a panicky moment Faustino imagined that she had somehow slipped away, abandoned him. Imprisoned him because his own death was to be part of this terrible thing. But no; he heard her move, saw the silhouette of her head block out half of the window.

"Prima, for Chrissakes let me out. I think I'm going to be sick."

"No, you ain't. Be of good heart, Señor Paul. It almost over now."

The man whom Lucas had shot, the man slumped clownishly against the wall, was named Benno, and he knew he was going to die. He'd been in the business for a good while, and he knew the signs. He'd gone and gotten himself killed, just like he'd always known he would, always been told he would. He'd stayed still and quiet dealing with the pain for what felt like a year now, thinking that maybe he might come through and get fixed up, but no, it wasn't going to happen. It wasn't that kind of a situation.

Too cold now, anyway. The warmth had all run out of him and couldn't be gotten back. He was lying in a pool of it. And the word for the cold that was filling him up was *disappointment*. Disappointment so deep it could never have been imagined.

He opened his eyes. It was such a huge thing to do that he was surprised nobody heard it happen and shot him again.

One eye had gone blind. No, it was the hood thing slid over it. Shit. Thinking was so slow it was like laying bricks. The eye he could see with was on the same side as the hand that held the gun. There it was, down at the end of his arm. Beyond that, there was all this crazy crisscross of light, like car headlights in the rain.

Car headlights in the rain was beautiful. He nearly remembered something, but then it went.

In among the dazzle, there was the guy in the white. Not the old guy they'd brought with them. He'd gone. No, the other sonofabitch in fancy dress who'd come from nowhere and got him killed.

Sound came on now. Chanting. The guy in white. Chanting at the soccer kid. Who was, come to think of it, why he'd ended up here dying in the first place.

It was going to be the biggest thing ever just to lift the gun out of the puddle. Come on, hand. Come on.

The hand wasn't listening. Like it didn't belong to him anymore.

He wanted to give up. Besides, there was a kind of pulp in the middle of his body that wanted to come out of his mouth, and he needed to deal with that.

Then, hey, look, the hand lifted. It was wearing a red sticky glove he'd never seen before, and it had the gun in it. It all lined up: arm, hand, gun, crosshairs of light, the back of the man in white.

Pull the damn trigger. Pull, damn you to hell.

Something greater than physical tiredness had possessed Faustino. There was a limit to the number of brutal and irrational things a civilized man could put up with, and he'd gone beyond it. His world had shrunk to this nasty dark space. It wasn't just a nightmare anymore; it was an outrage. It had numbed him. He sat for a while on the chair, slumped, his forearms on his knees, his head hanging. He thought about lighting his last cigarette, as a small act of defiance, then decided he couldn't be bothered.

The only sound from the shrine was Bakula's chanting, rising and falling, pausing, rising and falling. Faustino ached, almost prayed, for it to stop. Wearily he got up and went to the window. When he'd last looked, Brujito had been on the floor at Bakula's feet, twisting about and moaning gibberish in a horrible way; now he'd calmed down and gotten onto his knees. He looked happily drunk, swaying slightly from side to side and sort of hiccuping. Maybe this whole lunatic business really was coming to an end.

Then everything went mad again.

Someone—Mateo? Yes, Mateo—yelled, *"Lucas!"* Lucas began to turn away from the shrine, lifting his hand with the gun in it. A loud bang came from somewhere down to Faustino's right, close to the vestry wall. Then both Lucas and Mateo were firing in that direction, four shots, maybe five. They came all in one deafening stammer.

Prima screamed something and groped her way along to

the door, yanked at the bolt, dragged the door open; then she was out of the room and walking through the candlelight toward Bakula and Brujito. It seemed that they had done something to make her angry, because she was shaking her hands beside her face and saying, "No, no."

For some reason that had nothing to do with making a conscious decision, Faustino also went to the door. There was a short drop on the other side that he failed to take account of. He tottered forward, stumbled over the body of the false priest, and fell. The hand he put down to save himself slid through the line of congealed blood and came to rest on the salt. Frightened and embarrassed, he got to his feet, ineffectually wiping his hand on the front of the slithery black jacket. A few feet away, the hoodless guy was curled up on the ground with his arms wrapped around his head. He was making small noises like a kicked dog. On the far side of him, Mateo and Lucas were standing over the other man, who was too awful to look at. The air was full of the bad-egg smell of shooting.

Over in the shrine itself, both Bakula and Ricardo were kneeling, awkwardly embracing like two inexperienced lovers. Bakula was resting his head on Ricardo's left shoulder. Neither of them knew what to do with their hands. Bakula's were tucked awkwardly in front of him. Ricardo's made tentative attempts to settle on Bakula's back but couldn't, perhaps because of the dark stain that was slowly spreading on the white shirt. Juan stood in the background, bracing himself against one of the shrine's uprights. The arm with the gun at the end of it hung by his side. He was looking down at the floor, desolate.

The gunfire might have made Faustino temporarily deaf, because only now did he become aware of the angry persistent hiss coming from the television set. The screen had dissolved into seething black-and-red pixels around two flickering white disks.

"Edson? Pai?" It was Prima's voice.

Bakula must have heard her, because a second or two later his head lifted and his body moved slowly back, away from Ricardo's. He raised his hands and stared at them, apparently fascinated by their redness.

Lucas said, "Oh, man," and then he and Mateo put their guns away and went over, and because he didn't know what else to do, Faustino followed them, three big dark moths heading for the light.

Prima was kneeling beside Edson and her brother now. "Pai? Please. *Please*. Is it done? Is Rico OK?"

Bakula did not speak. He seemed to be holding his breath. Ricardo was staring at him, drop-lipped and wide-eyed. Faustino had seen that expression on the boy's face before, on a video. It was, in a word, stupid. There was a good deal of blood on the front of his shirt.

Prima reached out and gripped Bakula's shoulder. "Pai! Please!"

Mateo said, "Aw, Prima, girl. C'mon now. Leave it."

She lifted her face to him. There was so much pain and ferocity in her eyes that he shrugged and looked away.

Bakula turned his head toward Prima. His eyes sought and found focus, and he smiled. It was a smile of enormous gentleness. His teeth were outlined in red. He said something that Faustino could not catch. Blood gathered inside his lower lip and spilled out where it was notched, running down the scar. Prima closed her eyes and nodded; it seemed she had heard what she wanted to hear. Bakula was trembling violently now but reached forward and took hold of Ricardo's shoulders, pulling him close, and kissed the boy on both cheeks, leaving a daub of red on each. Then he fell sideways against Prima. She struggled to bear his weight. His legs went flat on the floor, and his head slid down onto her lap.

Mateo knelt, tearing open the front of Bakula's shirt.

"Jesus," Lucas murmured.

Faustino caught sight of the exit wound and looked away, trying not to retch, but not before he'd glimpsed a raised pink cross, the welt of a healed burn, on the front of the man's shoulder.

Mateo leaned closer. "Edson? Edson, can you hear me, man? There anything you wan' us to do?"

But Bakula's eyes were going out; they were already semiopaque, like lightly frosted glass. It surprised Faustino that the *pai* had the strength to speak, but he did: a few words in some dead or distant language. He raised his hands slightly, cupping the fingers, touching some imaginary face, perhaps. His chin was bearded in blood. The last word was a cry that was harsh yet joyous, a fierce benediction.

"Blessing!"

The silence that followed was more profound than it should have been. It took Faustino a few seconds to realize that the hiss from the television set had ceased and the screen was a blank gray rectangle.

He walked away between the guttering candles, fumbling in his pocket for the creased cigarette packet. He paused in the doorway and looked back. Dimly illuminated, framed by the timbers of the shrine, the scene was a familiar one. The dead man slumped in the woman's lap, the disheveled white garments, the displayed wound, the dark huddle of grieving Apostles. He'd seen it many times, hung on many walls, during his priest-haunted childhood. Had turned his back on it, repelled and unbelieving. Had fled from it through the rooms and years and pages of his life.

He stood studying it for a moment or two, then lit up.

EPILOGUE: FAUSTINO'S CROSS

Paul Faustino was trekking across the glossily tiled lobby of the Hotel San Francesco (wondering yet again why a hotel lobby needed a grand piano) when the woman at the desk called his name.

"*Signore Faustino? Scusi, Signore. Telefono.*"

She held the phone in the air and pointed at it, perhaps imagining that it was an unfamiliar object to a South American.

"*Grazie.*" It was one of the nine Italian words that Faustino knew.

"Paul. It's Carmen. How's Rome?"

"Old, and very expensive."

"I imagine you must blend in perfectly, then."

It was the first time in his life he'd heard his boss make anything resembling a joke. He was so startled that he missed the beginning of her next sentence.

"Sorry, what? There's a delay on the line."

"I said, excellent news. After six weeks of hassling by our lawyers, the San Juan Prosecutor's Office has agreed to let us publish your account of the Brujito business. We got them on the public interest angle, in the end. It's likely to be four months or more before Varga and company come to trial."

"Ah. OK. That's good."

"*Good?* It's a damn sight better than *good,* Paul. We've busted a gut on this thing. Are you all right?"

Faustino cleared his throat and brisked himself up a bit. "Yes. Sorry. I guess I just feel a bit out of the loop. No, that's great, Carmen."

"Yes, it is. Your friend Sergeant—sorry—*Lieutenant* Artur Fillol has been very helpful, by the way."

"Yeah. I imagine he must enjoy having us to talk to. It must get lonely, being an honest cop in San Juan. I'm glad he got a promotion, though."

"He didn't," Carmen said. "He was already a lieutenant. In the Federal Office of Investigation. He was planted in Varga's branch of the SJDP almost a year ago. Seems there was already a bad smell coming from there."

"Well, well, well. Any other news? How's Prima de Barros?"

"The girl? She's OK, so far as I know. Fillol's still got two of his men up there in Santo Whatsit. Witness protection, but it also keeps the competition away. Incidentally, did you

252

know that the phony priest guy, the one Bakula strangled, was her uncle? Her aunt's brother? Paul? Are you still there?"

"Yes, sorry. No, I didn't know that. She didn't tell me that."

"It's a great angle, isn't it? We're making it into a pretty strong background story to the main piece. Get some family tragedy into the mix."

"Carmen, I don't . . . I think we should discuss this."

But she wasn't listening. She'd put her hand over the phone. Faustino could hear muffled conversation; she was talking to someone else.

"Carmen?"

"Paul, sorry. This will interest you, I think. The team for the exhibition game against Brazil has just been announced. Ricardo de Barros is on it."

"Ah. Good. That's very good."

"And perfect timing for us. I've always said that God is a *Nación* reader. Now, what's your schedule?"

"Well, I'm having dinner with Luiz Falcao, who was assistant manager at Unita during Gato's time here, then—"

"No, no. What I meant, Paul, is when are you coming back?"

Here it comes, Faustino thought.

"Um, Madrid Sunday, home Monday. Late. Why?"

"We're putting the story out as a twelve-page special supplement the weekend after next. I've had a couple of people doing the background stuff, but the meat of it is the transcript of your tape. However, there are some gaps, and one or two things we don't really understand."

Faustino almost laughed. "You and me both, Carmen."

There was a short icy silence that had nothing to do with the time it takes words to bounce off a satellite.

"Yes, well. Frankly, Paul, a good deal of it seems . . . Never mind. We can discuss it when you come into the office on Tuesday."

"What? Hell's teeth, Carmen. I'll be spent. Jet-lagged. Come on."

"It doesn't have to be early. Nine thirty will do."

Faustino sighed and leaned back against the reception desk. The door onto the street opened, and the San Francesco's doorman guided a smartly dressed blind man toward the grand piano.

"Paul?"

"Yeah, Carmen. May I tell you something? Sometimes, just sometimes, you are the last person I want to hear from."

"It breaks my heart to hear you say that, Paul. See you on Tuesday. And, Paul? Take care. You don't seem your old self."

Faustino's lack of a sense of direction was legendary among his colleagues. He could get lost in a barrel, they'd say, after he'd been found once again wandering the bland labyrinth of the Nación building, bemoaning the inhumanity of modern architects. So it was not surprising—even to Faustino himself—that within thirty minutes of leaving the hotel, he had no idea where he was. He could have taken a taxi, but he had been told that strolling through Rome on a summer evening was one of life's great pleasures. He had a street map in his pocket but refused to look at it; he didn't want to be mistaken for a mere tourist. For the same reason, he refused to ask for directions. Not that he would know how. Then there was the problem that, to his New World eyes, all those damn great Renaissance buildings looked the same. So the upshot was that he'd gotten his bridges muddled up, crossed the Tevere at the wrong place, and ended up in a piazza far from the one he'd been aiming for.

All at once he was overwhelmed by just how lost, how alone, he was. He'd experienced the same thing a number of times in the last few weeks. It was like a swift gathering, an inrush, of shadows, shadows that were almost memories. Of a little boy finding a doctor and a priest talking quietly outside his mother's bedroom. Of looking up from play and finding everybody gone, the garden silent and inexplicably enormous. Of understanding for the first time the vast and terrible perspective of the stars. *Lost* was a poor word for such a feeling. Rather, it was as if all directions had been obliterated, the agreed limits of the world abolished. It made him want to beg like a dog for consolation.

It occurred to him that he might be looking a little peculiar. And yes, a young couple—so beautiful, both of them—watched him as they passed. For a dreadful moment, it seemed they might stop and ask him if he was all right. If he needed help. He tugged the map from his pocket and fumbled it open. Useless. It was badly printed, blurry. Or could it be that he needed glasses suddenly? Anyway, maps were pointless if you didn't know where you were in the first place. He was pretty sure he could find his way back to the river; if he walked straight on for a bit and took a right, he would come to it and get his bearings.

He would have gone past the church — wouldn't even have noticed that it was yet another church — if it hadn't been for the interesting pair of human skulls that flanked its doorway. They were not particularly scary, as skulls go. The sculptor had carved them with open mouths and immense eye sockets so that, in this evening light, they looked like two shocked old ladies wearing sunglasses. Oddly, they sprouted uplifted wings resembling torn palm leaves, and dangling things rather like neckties made of flowers and small clusters of fruit. As a result, they struck Faustino as being both morbid and luxuriantly tropical. Perhaps he experienced a moment of homesickness, but for whatever reason, after the slightest of hesitations, he went inside.

The gloom was a welcome relief from the hot amber and ocher of the outside world. His eyes liked it. He couldn't be sure, but he thought the place was empty. There was a flickering glow ahead and to the right of him, and he headed for that, trying not to bump into anything sacred.

The uncertain light came from three narrow metal shelves hung with swags and stalactites of stiffened wax. Nine small flames burned among many white stubs with drowned and blackened wicks. He stared at them for a whole minute, then looked around until he found the box of short cheap candles and the slot for cash. He took a five-euro note from his pocket and wasted a few seconds trying to work out what that was in real money. Enough, probably. He put the note into the slot and took a candle. For Max Salez, the godless jerk. *Our jerk.* He lit it with his cigarette lighter and pressed it down onto one of the dead candles on the middle shelf. Then, why the hell not, he helped himself to a second one. For Edson Bakula. He stood watching the flames until they steadied. After a while he started to feel conspicuous, so he knelt.

He had absolutely no idea how to pray. He had only a few half-remembered phrases that had somehow survived the process of forgetting, of erasure. Besides, prayer was not an act; it was a place. It was the place his mother had retreated to, leaving him behind because he didn't know the way. He'd watched her go, out of the corner of his eye. He'd waited for her to come back, and she did. Until the day she didn't.

Well, that was that. He was about to get to his feet, when he realized he was not alone.

A very old lady was kneeling not far from him. Her eyes were closed, and she was speaking silently in a fast peaceful rhythm that was somehow like the way marathon runners run when they've hit the right pace for the distance. Now and again she paused and crossed herself: high, low, left, right. He watched her; then suddenly she was watching him. She smiled. She had a gold tooth in the upper right jaw. She nodded encouragement, and because nothing else would do, Faustino crossed himself: high, low, right, left. Then he got to his feet and made his way out into the pulverizing light of Rome.

At that same moment, several hours earlier (on account of the way we mark the slow ruthless turning of the world), on the Deportivo San Juan practice field, El Brujito tried to fake out Braca, his team captain, failed, and fell on his ass.

Braca took the ball on for a few yards and then put his foot on it. He looked back at the boy, worried. After what had happened, you couldn't tell how he'd react. The newsflash of the kid getting out of the helicopter into the glare of the TV lights, still covered in blood. The hell that broke loose. How do you get over that? How do you begin to forget?

But look at the Little Sorcerer sitting there, face up to the clouds and laughing. Laughing, praise God.

Four miles away from the field, at the top of The Pillory, a white-haired man wearing an England soccer jersey stood shackled to a wall. The exposed parts of his body were the color of broiled lobster. He was a good sport, though; he adopted appropriately tortured poses while other members of the tour group (including his wife) took photographs.

The guide waited. He was a slightly built, medium-skinned man whose hair was showing early hints of gray. He wore sunglasses with rather snazzy red-and-black mottled frames. His neat mustache and beard were perhaps intended to disguise, but only accentuated, the scar that ran down from the notch in his lower lip. When the photographers had finished, he continued his spiel.

"The terrace we are standing on is called the Old Slave Market. However, the truth is slightly more complicated."

AUTHOR'S NOTE

I've heard it said, and seen it written, that the Paul Faustino novels are "set in Brazil." This isn't true. They are set in an imaginary South American country. I'm happy to confess that when I wrote the first one, *Keeper*, I'd never been to South America. So I had no choice but to imagine. I did no real research. The only sourcebook I used was called something like *Rain Forests of the World*. It had lots of really useful photographs in it. I never got around to reading the text.

When I started work on *The Penalty*, I was intending to go about things in much the same way. That is, I was going to make it all up. Then my wife, Ellie, started to mention — about five times a day — that she'd always wanted to go to South America. So there was nothing to do but go. As a result of that monthlong trip, the setting of *The Penalty* is,

I guess, a little more "authentic" than in *Keeper*. Yes, there are bits of Brazil in this book; there are bits of other places too. But Faustino's country, El Brujito's country, exists only in my imagination—and in yours, perhaps.

One of the things that impressed and fascinated me about South America was the way that African culture—the culture of millions of victims of the barbaric slave trade—continues to survive and flourish in certain areas. In particular, religions that originated in western Africa remain powerful and influential. Learning about these changed the book I was writing. (Originally, Paracleto was just a ghostly voice whispering through the text. Then he started to grow and develop in ways that surprised me.) But, just as the country in *The Penalty* is fictitious, so is the religion that I call "Veneration." I have taken underlying ideas from religions such as Bahian Candomblé, but the symbols, rituals, and names of spirits in Veneration are my inventions. I hope.

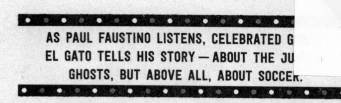

AS PAUL FAUSTINO LISTENS, CELEBRATED G⬚
EL GATO TELLS HIS STORY — ABOUT THE JU⬚
GHOSTS, BUT ABOVE ALL, ABOUT SOCCER.

★ "This stirring adventure . . . defies
expectations. . . . Both lyrical and gripping."
—*Kirkus Reviews* (starred review)

"Readers scrambling for soccer stories
will be begging for this captivating tale."
—*Bulletin of the Center for Children's Books*

Available in hardcover, paperback, and audio and as an e-book

🐞 🌿 🍃 🌿 🐞 🌿 **www.candlewick.com** 🌿 🍃 🌿 🐞 🌿 🍃

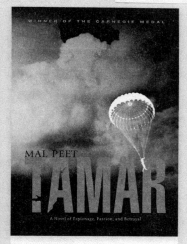